QUAKE!

QUAKE!

A NOVEL

JOE COTTONWOOD

AN
APPLE
PAPERBACK

SCHOLASTIC INC.
New York Toronto London Auckland Sydney

ISBN 0-590-22233-3

22 21 20 19 18 17 16 15 14   4 5 6 7 8 9/0

Printed in the U.S.A.   40

*This book is dedicated to the hardy
children of the Santa Cruz Mountains,
small heroes one and all.*

QUAKE!

TUESDAY, OCTOBER 17, 1989

I hadn't seen Jennie for five years. We used to live side by side in San Jose. I remember how she used to trap mice in a cage — in secret, because her father was trying to exterminate them — and give them birthday parties. She would bake chocolate cupcakes, and I'd bring a crumb of bacon wrapped in tissue as a present, and then she and I and the mouse would devour the goodies. After the party, she'd release the mouse in her backyard. I'm sure it moved right back into her house, hoping to be caught again.

When I got a squirmy little golden retriever pup, Jennie baked chocolate chip cookies and fed them, one by one, to the puppy, who ate until her belly bulged out and then fell asleep on Jennie's foot, occasionally giving off contented little chocolate burps. From then on, that dog was ready to be Jennie's friend for life. So was I.

Jennie in my memory was a chunky, pixie-haired, animal-loving, happy-go-lucky chocoholic.

Now we were fourteen years old.

The moment she stepped out of the car, I saw a different Jennie: long hair gathered in a purple scrunchie, purple eye shadow that looked like a bruise, a purple shirt tied to reveal a purple tattoo of a guitar on her belly — on second glance, not a real tattoo but the press-on kind. She was wearing headphones.

"Hi, Franny."

"Hi, Jennie."

We hugged. It was a leaning forward, lightly touching hug. When my head was next to hers, I could hear music in her headphones.

"*God*, you've like totally changed!" she said.

"*I've* changed? You look so — "

"Your hair's like *red*."

"Jennie, it's always been red."

"I thought it was brown."

How could she forget the color of my hair?

We'd been best friends all our lives — until our world cracked apart. Jennie's parents had divorced, and Jennie had moved with her mother to Pomona. Then I moved with my family to the mountains — to Loma Prieta, halfway between San Jose and Santa Cruz — to an old shoe of a cabin where I had to share a room with my brother.

We'd tried writing letters, but they came less and less often. Jennie's last letter almost two years ago had said:

I think of our life together in San Jose as a time when everything was simple and happy.

st forever. Now I know
. And nothing lasts for-

This was a new Jennie. I didn't know how to talk to her. My eyes fell to the tattoo on her belly. Inside the guitar were the letters BIG UGLY.

"What's Big Ugly?" I asked.

Jennie looked at me with surprise. But she didn't say anything.

Louder, I said, "What — or who — is Big Ugly?"

Without a word, Jennie handed me the headphones. The wire stretched from her waist.

I listened to a sound like somebody stomping on watermelons. And a voice that was a raw shout.

I handed back the headphones and asked, "Is Big Ugly a person? Or a band?"

"Franny . . ." Her voice was a whine. "Haven't you seen them on TV?"

"No, I can't."

Suddenly Jennie looked worried. "Don't you get — like — cable? MTV?"

"The thing is . . . you see . . . we don't have a television."

Now Jennie looked sick.

"Are you all right?"

"What are we going to *do*?" Jennie wailed.

3

I'd thought we might talk. Catch up on our lives. Reminisce. Maybe catch mice.

People change, I told myself. Lives change. Kids grow. Parents divorce. Families move. Nothing is permanent. Maybe that was why in school I was feeling more and more drawn to science, where the laws don't change. Earth is earth. Rock is rock.

As I was standing awkwardly outside with Jennie, wondering what to say, Lara came out of the house, barking. Lara was the squirmy golden retriever puppy whom Jennie had befriended with chocolate chip cookies, years ago. Now Lara was a ninety-pound dog, lazy as a shaggy golden boulder, but she had bestirred herself to come out and woof at this stranger.

"Is that Lara?" Jennie asked. "She's totally *huge*. Why is she barking? Doesn't she recognize me?"

Lara definitely did not recognize her. I'm not sure I would have recognized Jennie, either, if I hadn't been expecting her.

"Lara! It's me. Like — remember?"

Woof woof.

Jennie unzipped a pocket of her overnight bag and pulled out a Reese's Peanut Butter Cup. Lara stopped barking and sat. Her tail wagged back and forth in the dust like a hairy broom. Jennie unwrapped the Reese's and held it out.

4

Delicately, with her front teeth, Lara removed the peanut butter cup from Jennie's fingers. Then — gulp — it was gone. And once again, Lara was Jennie's friend for life.

I was relieved. Here, at least, was one part of Jennie that hadn't changed. I hoped we had some chocolate in the kitchen. Maybe if I gave some to Jennie, she'd be my friend for life again, too.

My father had gone into the house. Now he returned to the car. "Got to run," he said. "Wish me luck. Go, Giants!" With a spray of gravel, he launched out of the driveway.

My father was a diehard Giants fan. So was Jennie's mom. And that was why Jennie and I were finally back together again for a couple of nights: The Giants were in the World Series. My father and mother plus Jennie's mother were all going to the game at Candlestick Park. Jennie and her mom had flown up from Pomona. My mom took Jennie's mom to a restaurant while my dad drove Jennie to our house. Jennie would stay with me and help baby-sit for my little brother, Sidney, until our parents got home, which with ballpark traffic would be very late at night.

As my father drove away, Sidney came out of the house.

"Is that — like — little Sidney?" Jennie exclaimed. When she'd last seen him, he was two years old.

"What's that on your stomach?" Sidney asked.

"Tattoo."

"It looks like a bullet hole."

Sidney is living proof of genetic mutation. There's no other explanation for how he and I could come from the same parents. Sidney was the reason that my father gave our perfectly good nineteen-inch Sony Trinitron to the Salvation Army.

Sidney liked cop shows and war movies (though he wasn't allowed to watch them). Sidney played violent video games (in other kids' houses). Sidney kept asking my dad to take him to a junkyard so he could see all the smashed cars. Sidney said that his second-grade teacher was made of reconstructed liposuction. She was a sweet old lady who happened to be obese. Sidney called her Mrs. Lipo.

Sidney was precocious, but he gave me the creeps. Sometimes in the middle of the night, I saw Sidney get up and watch forbidden, bloody TV shows with the sound turned off. It seemed to relax him — like a mug of warm milk.

One night, a couple of months ago, my dad caught him.

My dad was a medic in Vietnam. He tried to

make Sidney understand that blood and gore were
real, that it happened to real people, that it was
horrible. He told Sidney about a man who had his
right arm blown off, who picked it up with his left
hand and carried it to my dad with a dazed look
on his face and asked, "Do you want this?"

And Sidney said, "Cool."

My dad told Sidney about bodies burned like
overdone marshmallow, about intestines dripping
out into a man's lap, about body bags and helicopter evacuations under fire.

And Sidney said, "Wow."

That's when my dad decided to get rid of our
television.

Sidney pretended he didn't care. I noticed,
though, that he was thrashing in bed at night at
times when he used to get up and watch the silent,
bloody shows that so strangely settled him down.

For me it was weird for a week or two, not being
able to switch on the TV when I got bored. Pretty
soon, though, I found I was spending more time
making earrings — sort of a hobby of mine — more
time taking walks with Lara and running into
friends of mine — in particular happening to pass
the house of a boy named Eric who always just
happened to be coming out of the door as Lara and
I were passing by and just happened to feel like

7

taking the time to chat — and I wasn't bored at all. In fact, I think watching the tube had *made* me bored. Television wasn't the solution. It had been the problem.

Sometimes, though, when my friends started talking about a show they'd seen the night before, I felt left out. They made fun of commercials I'd never heard. It was as if they had a secret language.

Giving up TV was more of a sacrifice for my dad. Without the tube, he couldn't watch the World Series at home. But then he got tickets. And so I was baby-sitting for Sidney. And Jennie.

At least, it felt as if I was her sitter. First thing in the house, I'd check the kitchen for chocolate.

Jennie was moping. She said, "I've got a feeling that there is like totally *nothing* to do here."

"Like, totally," Sidney said.

"Don't make fun of the way I talk."

"Like, okay."

"Shut up."

"Totally." But he didn't shut up. Instead, he sang her a song. Sidney always had songs, and I was never sure which ones he made up and which ones he'd heard from someone else. This one went to the tune of "Joy to the World," the Christmas carol:

> *"Joy to the world!*
> *Jennie is dead.*
> *They barbecued her head.*
> *Oh, where is her body?*
> *They flushed it down the potty.*
> *And round and round it goes,*
> *And round and round it goes,*
> *And rou-ound, and rou-ow-ound,*
> *   and round it goes."*

"That is totally dis*gus*ting," Jennie said.
Sidney turned to me and sang:

> *"Joy to the world!*
> *There goes Franny's jaw.*
> *They sliced it with a chainsaw.*
> *Oh, see her great big bottom-us,*
> *Looks like a hippopotamus.*
> *And bouncy bounce it goes,*
> *And bouncy bounce it goes . . ."*

I tried to ignore him. I knew that if I responded in any way, he'd start calling me Franny-Big-Fanny.

I *don't* have a big fanny.

I walked into the house, which meant walking

9

up a gangplank to an opening with no door. We were adding on to the cabin. The carpenters had gone home for the day.

"Like, how do you live here?" Jennie asked.

"It's crowded," I said. "But it's temporary."

Quickly I checked the kitchen. Alas, no chocolate.

We lived in the old part of the house: two bedrooms built as a summer cabin fifty years ago. In one room Jennie could see a bunk bed with the top half neatly made — mine — and the bottom — Sidney's — looking as if it had been the site of a dogfight.

"Where will I sleep?" Jennie asked.

"I thought we'd share my bed."

We used to share beds. We used to be a lot smaller, too. And we used to have rooms of our own without a little brother in the bottom bunk.

This whole visit was turning into a disaster. We should have waited until the house was finished. But then, the World Series wouldn't wait. And Jennie would still be a stranger.

The carpenters were adding four new rooms and a deck. It still wouldn't be a large house, but it was all my folks could afford. Anyway, compared to the two rooms we were crammed into, the addition seemed immense. So far, only stud walls divided the inside, but soon one of those stud walls would be mine in a room that would be mine where I wouldn't have to listen to Sidney making rude noises with his hand in his armpit when I was trying to sleep. In my room I'd have a work table where I could make earrings out of gems and wire.

Our house was on a ridge of the mountain Loma Prieta in the Santa Cruz Mountains. From the new deck you could see across the canyon to hill after rolling hill all the way to the Pacific Ocean. It's gorgeous. I love this spot. Sunset is my favorite time. The ridges grow violet and hazy in the distance; fog snakes up the valleys; clouds turn pink, then darken to purple; the sun turns into a soft orange globe that flattens as it settles into the water. My father said he'd rather have a large view than a large house, and that's exactly what we had.

Jennie was checking out the view, standing at a brand-new window with a big masking tape X stuck on the glass from corner to corner. Lara lay down at her feet.

"Why do they always — like — tape up new windows?" Jennie asked. Suddenly she reached a hand toward my face and touched my ear. "Neat earrings. What is that?"

Aha! Something we could talk about.

"Agate," I said. "I found it on a great little beach

11

that practically nobody knows about. I made the earrings myself. I make a lot of — "

"Neat," Jennie said, but her eyes went out of focus as some sound in the headphones required her full attention.

I wished Sidney would pour maple syrup into those headphones.

Jennie stood at the window staring moodily out between the lines of tape, tapping her foot to something only she could hear.

Sidney was packing sawdust into a pile and shaping it into a volcano. He was lying on the plywood floor of the space that was going to be our new living room. The walls were bare studs with plywood on the outside. There was the wet, sappy smell of freshly cut lumber and the chemical smell of plywood glue. Scattered around on the floor were dropped nails and empty tubes of caulk.

As Sidney packed his volcano of sawdust, he went on quietly singing his awful song.

He was too young to know what he was saying. He couldn't imagine a head on a barbecue spit, roasting slowly over a fire. He couldn't see bloody body parts swirling down a toilet bowl. Or could he? I couldn't believe he would sing such a song if he knew what he was actually saying. But if he made it up, wouldn't he have to know what it meant?

"Sidney? Did you make up that song?"

"Somebody had to."

"Did you?"

"Hey, Franny. Watch this."

Sidney jumped up and down on the plywood floor. With each stomp of his feet, the volcano shook. Little landslides of sawdust ran down the sides of his mountain; the cone collapsed; cracks formed and disappeared.

Lara groaned at the stomping, rolled over, and rested her head on Jennie's foot.

Sidney got down on his knees and started shaping it all over again. As he was rounding out the cone, he ran his hand over something sharp — a tiny scrap of sheet metal that had mixed with the sawdust.

"Ow!"

He held up his palm.

"I'm *bleeding*."

It wasn't a crisis. But it was a cut.

Before I could move, Jennie had crossed the room and found the medicine cabinet in the bathroom. In a few seconds she returned with a washcloth, towel, and Band-Aid. Without a word she

13

wiped Sidney's palm clean, dried it, then placed the Band-Aid over the cut. She still had her headphones on.

This was the old Jennie, too. She used to bandage all her dolls. Her room had always looked like a hospital ward.

"Thank you," Sidney said sheepishly.

"You're totally welcome," Jennie said sincerely. And then she returned to her window, back to the sounds of her own private world, back, I suppose, to stomping watermelons.

Sidney studied the Band-Aid on his palm. He asked, "Has the baseball game started yet?"

I looked at the time on the microwave oven: 5:02 P.M.

"No, Sidney, not yet."

Suddenly Lara whined. She'd been lying stretched out between Jennie's feet with sawdust coating her fur like breadcrumbs on fried chicken. On a hot day like today, she could sleep from sunrise to sunset.

With the whine, Lara stood up. She slipped out from under Jennie, whimpered at us once, and cocked her head. I had the distinct impression that she was trying to tell us something.

"What is it, Lara?"

She seemed to be in pain. She flicked her ears

as if reacting to some sound. I couldn't hear anything. Then again she whined. With her tail between her legs she trotted across the floor, out the open doorframe, and down the gangplank.

I watched from the doorway. With her tail still tucked between her legs, Lara trotted through some Scotch broom — it's a brushy weed — and disappeared behind some blackberry bushes. I smelled sunbaked evergreen air. I loved that smell. It was the scent of the mountains in summer — though it was autumn. A hot day in autumn.

"She's hurt," Sidney said. He'd come to my side.

"Maybe a bee stung her," I said.

We both knew lazy Lara. We knew that little short of dynamite would move that dog out of the house, especially at a trot, on a hot day.

"Maybe she had a nightmare," Sidney said. "Maybe she dreamed she was drowning in a burning vat of vulture vomit."

I stared down at Sidney — the sweet brown eyes, the cowlicked hair. I said, "She's never heard of vulture vomit."

"Maybe she knows. Dogs know lots of things without anybody teaching them. It's instink."

"Instinct."

"Right."

So we had our warning. Lara knew something

15

was wrong. We just didn't know what. Sidney was thinking about burning vats of vulture vomit. I was enjoying the crisp hot evergreen scent and wondering why Lara had so suddenly seemed to be in pain — maybe it was indigestion from the peanut butter cup. Jennie was still inside at the new window, tapping her toe against a stud. Unknown to us, miles beneath our feet, the city of Los Angeles was about to move six feet closer to the city of San Francisco.

I stepped down the gangplank. Sidney stepped behind me. We moved toward where Lara had disappeared. The Scotch broom came up to my waist and to Sidney's chin.

Then it began.

5:04 P.M.

I heard it before I felt it. And I felt it before I saw it. I heard the roar of a freight train so close, I could have touched it — so close, it might be running me over — except we lived twenty miles from a railroad track.

The ground wobbled. It was like trying to stand on an air mattress on top of a swimming pool. I fell. I tried to break my fall with my hands and felt a sharp pain in my left wrist as it struck the ground — or rather, as the dirt came up and struck my hand, which was on the way down to meet it. It was confusing. Normally when you fall, that's it. You lie there until you're ready to get up. Instead, what was happening was that the ground wrenched upward and rolled me over twice out of the weeds. Then somehow I managed to steady myself on my hands and knees with the earth still wobbling underneath. Sidney was thrown beside me. He lay on his stomach. We both looked out at the house, the canyon, the hills.

I was scared. I'd felt earthquakes before. But never like this.

You could see the land move. It looked like waves on the ocean, surging down the side of the mountain, rippling the trees. Below us on the road a car was bouncing up and down. The door flew open and a woman was thrown — or threw herself — onto the asphalt. A boulder the size of a file cabinet broke off the hillside and rolled to the road, hopped over the woman, and came down on the car with a crunch of metal and shattering of windshield.

If a boulder came at Sidney and me, I didn't know if we could get out of the way.

High-voltage wires strung between steel poles across the canyon were slapping together in the air, shooting showers of sparks. The tall redwood trees were whipping back and forth, and as I watched, the top of the tallest tree snapped right off.

If a tree fell on us — or a power line — we would die. We couldn't move. We couldn't stand up.

Our old stone chimney peeled off the house and crashed in a heap. Windows popped. Glass sprayed like water. Through the hole where the chimney had been, I saw shelves spilling their books and vases and photos.

At the side of the house, the door to the water heater closet flew open. The water heater fell out, and for a weird moment it looked like a mummy falling out of a coffin. Behind it a flame shot to the

ceiling and then died as the gas pipe burst somewhere else along the line.

From our apple tree dozens of ripe Granny Smith
apples were dropping to the ground and then
bouncing like Ping-Pong balls.

Beyond our house farther up the ridge, I saw the
stilts of old Mr. Vanda's cabin snapping like dry
spaghetti. The cabin teetered, then sank to the
ground and slid, shuffling downhill like a big old
green turtle. The propane tank rolled loose. It followed the house down the hillside, tumbling and
rolling like a football. Suddenly it struck an out-
cropping of rock and bounced. It was airborne. The
long white tank hung in the air for what seemed
an eternity flipping end over end, came down on
the rocks — and exploded with a BOOM and a ball
of flame.

Then everything stopped.

Just as suddenly as it started, it ended. I felt as
if we had shaken for hours, but I knew it was
probably less than a minute.

And in that minute, my whole world had shaken
apart.

Sidney grabbed my leg and held on for dear life.
I stayed on my hands and knees, afraid for the
moment to stand.

19

Jennie appeared at the open doorway of the house. "Are you sure those carpenters know what they're *doing*?" she shouted. She had a cut on the side of her neck, probably from flying glass.

"It wasn't the carpenters, Jen."

She was looking around. "Oh, wow," she said.

It was quiet. So quiet, it was eerie. A huge brown dust cloud was rising over everything. The trees had stopped moving. The power lines had stopped slapping. The apples had stopped bouncing. The woman was running down the road, her car still under the boulder. Mr. Vanda's house had slid out of sight. The circle of fire around the propane tank swirled, spread wider over the rocks, and then quickly died down as the gas was spent, replaced by black smoke rising from the scorched rocks and one burning bush.

Jennie jumped the few feet down from the doorway to the ground. The gangplank had fallen away. Blood was dribbling down her neck. It wasn't pulsing as it would from an artery, but it sure was bleeding.

Below our house and across the road, an old shed — rotten, termite-infested, waiting to fall down — still stood as if no earthquake had happened. How did it survive?

"Is everybody dead?" Sidney asked.

"No," I said.

"Rats," Sidney said.

I looked at him. He had to be joking. How could he at a time like this? If he could joke about it, he didn't get it. But if he asked if everybody was dead, then he did realize what had just happened. Sidney was a puzzle to me. I noticed that his eyes were wide as plums, and then I knew that yes, Sidney got it. Probably my eyes were just as wide. I could feel my heart thumping in my chest — thumping so hard I could *hear* it.

"Is Jennie dying?" Sidney asked.

"Why would I be dying?" Jennie asked.

"Because you slit your throat."

Jennie put her hand to her neck. She pulled her fingers away, covered with blood. "Oh, wow," she said. For an instant her eyes glanced around, searching.

I was feeling faint. I hate blood.

Jennie untied the bottom of her shirt and with a ferocious jerk ripped it halfway around the hem. She couldn't reach in back.

"Help me, Fran," she said.

I ripped it the rest of the way around.

Jennie wrapped the torn-off shirt bottom twice around her neck, but she couldn't see what she was doing.

21

"Am I covering it, Fran?"

"Not quite."

"Help me."

We used to play hospital back in San Jose where we'd wrap each other from head to toe in gauze. This was different, though. Bright scarlet blood was smearing over my fingers, making them slippery as oil as I moved the purple bandage into place. I was feeling sick.

"Does it look bad, Fran?"

"I can't tell. Geez, I'm getting blood all over my — "

"Don't worry. I don't have AIDS."

"I wasn't worried, Jen."

"Well, you *should*."

When we'd played hospital back in San Jose, we'd never worried about AIDS. We'd never heard of it.

"The stupid window like exploded all over me. I'm lucky it didn't hit an eye. Pull it tight, now."

I tugged on the ends of the bandage. "Am I choking you?"

"Not quite. Pull tighter."

I pulled. "Can you breathe?"

"Barely. Now tie it."

I made a square knot.

"Is it still bleeding, Fran?"

"A little, I think."

"Is it coming out of the bandage?"

"A bit. When you talk. It slides. Stop talking."

Sidney said, "Are you gonna die?"

"No."

"Does it hurt?"

"Shut up," I said. "Don't make her talk."

Sidney was standing right next to me, one hand grabbing my leg. Normally, he would never touch me.

I'd been too busy before, but now I was gradually becoming aware of a hissing sound — and the smell of gas. The odor jogged my memory into action. I thought of all the boring earthquake drills we'd had at school. Over and over we'd been told what to do. At home we made earthquake plans, too. We had a family meeting once a year on April 18, the anniversary of the big San Francisco earthquake of 1906. My great-grandfather, my mother's grandfather, had been in San Francisco on that day. My mother said that in hot weather — not in summer, but any other time of year when you don't expect a hot day — he'd sniff the air and look nervously around and mutter: "Earthquake weather." He said the big quake had happened on just such a hot day. A day like today.

In Great-grandfather's earthquake, more build-

23

ings were destroyed by fire than by shaking. He blamed the mayor. I never understood why.

At our family meetings, we'd sit around the dining table and review where to go while the earthquake was happening: Crawl under a table or stand under a doorway. Well, too late for that. We'd never discussed what to do if you were outside. Even if we'd been inside like Jennie, I doubt if we could have moved to a safe place with all the shaking going on. Then we talked about what to do next: Shut off the gas and the electricity. My father had made sure we all knew how to do it.

"Sidney. Let go of my leg. I have to move."

"Don't go!"

"I'm not leaving you. I have to shut off the gas."

Sidney followed, holding on to my blue jeans. Jennie walked beside me, putting on her headphones, turning the radio dial. "The stations are like totally *gone,*" she said.

"Don't talk," I said. The bandage had a dark spot over the cut, but it didn't look as if any more blood was running down from under it. I couldn't be sure because so much had already spread over her neck and been soaked up below the collar of her shirt.

Our propane tank was lying on its side. I stopped and stood twenty feet away. The air stank of gas.

"You can't go any closer," Sidney said.

24

Any spark would cause an explosion. If it exploded, it was near enough that it would set the house on fire — maybe start a wildfire that would burn up one whole side of the mountain. There was such a fire just four years ago before we moved in. Our old cabin, like a tough old redwood tree, had survived somehow.

"I've got to turn it off," I said.

"You'll barbecue your head," Sidney said. "And your toes. Your bellybutton. Everything."

"Don't make a spark. Let go of my leg."

"No."

"Sidney!"

"No."

He didn't want me to barbecue my head. He knew exactly what his song meant. And — surprise — he didn't want it to happen.

I had been through so many earthquake drills at school and so many meetings at home, it had been thoroughly driven into my head: After an earthquake, shut off the gas. I was brainwashed. Programmed like a robot.

Bound and determined to shut off that gas.

I grabbed Sidney's wrist and wrenched his hand off my leg, took a deep breath — nearly choked on the stink — and marched toward the tank.

I wondered if I would die, wondered if my entire

25

life would pass before my eyes in an instant. Then I thought: There's not that much yet that can pass before my eyes. I'm only fourteen years old. *I'm only a teenager*. The thought stuck in my mind. I'm only a teenager, why am I doing this? I'm only a teenager, what do I know? I'm only a teenager, why am I standing in a stinking cloud of gas?

My hand found the round handle, grasped it, turned. The turning made a scraping sound, like metal against metal. Would it make a spark? Would I suddenly be in the middle of a ball of flame — and barbecue my head? My toes? My bellybutton? Everything?

I turned and turned until it was tight. The hissing stopped. I was still holding my breath. Suddenly I could hold it no more and let it out in a rush. Then I sucked in a great lungful of horrible sulfurous-smelling gas and ran — and coughed — and ran — and fell coughing and gasping for fresh air at Sidney's and Jennie's sides.

Sidney immediately grabbed on to my leg again. Jennie took me by the shoulders.

"Let's get away from here," she said. "There's still gas in the air."

"Don't talk," I said between hacking coughs. "I'm all right."

Jennie pulled me up by the shoulders and guided

me — I was blinded by my coughing and my watery eyes. Sidney continued to cling to my blue jeans.

Air. Hot, dusty air. Gradually I got control of my lungs. I was panting as if I'd just run laps.

The earthquake drills at school, the meetings at home, ran like a mantra through my mind: Get under a table. Get under a doorframe. Shut off the gas. Shut off the electricity. Shut off the water if it leaks.

"The power!"

"Huh?" Jennie said.

I ran to the garage with Sidney running behind me, still holding on to my pants. Jennie walked after us, headphones on, one hand pressing the bandage over her neck. She seemed afraid of moving too fast for fear of jogging the cut open.

The electric meter wasn't moving. The line was dead. I wanted to flip the main breaker switch anyway, just to be sure. It was hard to move. Why do they make something so important so hard to use? I tried both hands at once. Got it.

"I found a radio station," Jennie said.

"Any news?" I asked.

"They say there was an earthquake."

"No kidding."

Inside the house I saw smoke.

"Sidney. Stay here."

I plucked his hand from my leg and attached it to Jennie's hand.

Was it safe to go into the house? Was it about to go shuffling down the hill as Mr. Vanda's had gone? There wasn't time to worry about it. The smoke was coming from the kitchen.

I jumped to the open doorframe. A tablesaw lay on its side. Glass had sprayed all over the plywood floor. Sidney's sawdust volcano had blown apart.

Inside the house, glass crunched under my shoes. Gray smoke curled out of the kitchen and thinned out as it spread.

Again I started to cough. My lungs were still sore from the gas. The smoke was coming from behind the stove. I couldn't see any flame. I went to the sink and turned the faucet handle. Nothing came out. Air sucked into the spout. From somewhere under the house came the sound of water gurgling out of a broken pipe. We had a fire extinguisher mounted on the wall next to the refrigerator — or where the refrigerator should have been. The whole refrigerator had walked several feet away. Its door had flown open and food had dumped on to the floor. I grabbed the red extinguisher, held my breath, leaned over the stove with my head

28

right in the rising smoke, and squeezed the handle.

Nothing happened.

I pulled my head back where I could breathe and where the smoke didn't burn my eyes as much and looked at the extinguisher. A red pin was stuck in the black handle. A tag said PULL OUT RING PIN. AIM NOZZLE AT BASE OF FIRE. SQUEEZE HANDLES. USE SIDE-TO-SIDE MOTION.

I pulled the pin. I took a deep breath, leaned over the stove again aiming at the space between the wall and the back of the stove, aiming down into the smoke, and squeezed.

It made a sound like whipped cream splatting out of a can. White powder — like chalk — shot out. I moved it from side to side and kept on squeezing until nothing more came out.

The smoke stopped rising. I'd buried it.

Something touched my pants. I jumped — but it was only Sidney. He'd followed me into the house.

Together we stared at the kitchen. It looked like raccoons had broken in, only a thousand times worse. The shelves had dumped. The cabinet doors had popped open, and everything had tumbled out. There was food and glass all over the counter and the floor: molasses, peanut butter, vinegar, sugar, wineglasses, honey, ketchup, flour, potatoes, graham crackers — all in a crunchy, gooey, sticky soup.

Briefly I glanced around the rest of the old part of the house. Nothing else was burning. And everything was on the floor, mixed with broken window glass and plaster that had popped off the walls. My bed was covered with little stones and wires from my jewelry-making supplies. My clothes dresser had fallen forward with the drawers sliding out. My aquarium was smashed. I didn't see any fish, but I knew they were dead. Sidney pushed some bedding out of the way and found his favorite stuffie: a fuzzy red parrot by the name of Squawk.

The phone was off the hook. I set it back, then listened for a dial tone. Nothing.

I felt little tremors through my shoes on the floorboards. Rafters creaked.

"Let's get out of here," I said.

The shutoff valve for the water was in a box in the ground. I lifted the cover, found the valve covered with daddy longlegs — brushed them away — one ran up my arm — shook it loose — tried to turn the valve handle — wouldn't budge — two hands — hard — oof — ah — shut it off. Sidney still clung to my blue jeans with one hand. With the other, he held Squawk. Jennie followed, listening to her headphones. I could still feel the thumping of my heart.

So far, I had been on automatic. After all the meetings, I'd known what to do. And I'd done it.

But now that I'd shut off the gas, the electricity, the water, now that I'd put out the fire, now that I was in charge of my little brother with a house that I was afraid to go into for fear that it would collapse, what was I supposed to do?

MR. VANDA

I sat down in the dirt. Sidney latched a finger into a belt loop on my jeans. He'd become permanently attached to me. He looked up at my face. "What are we gonna do?" he asked.

"Let me think a minute." What do I know? I'm only a teenager.

Suddenly it started again. I heard the rumble and roar. I grabbed Sidney and hugged him to me. Jennie fell to her knees. We shook. The house groaned. The trees cracked and swayed. More apples bounced. Somewhere across the canyon I heard another BOOM and knew that another propane tank had blown up.

Then just as suddenly, it stopped. It wasn't as bad as before. An aftershock.

I let go of Sidney. But he held on.

My mother and father were at Candlestick Park for the third game of the World Series. They were so far away, maybe they hadn't even felt the earthquake. Or if they felt a little shaking, would they realize what had happened here? Or if it had shaken just as badly there as it had here, would the stadium have collapsed? Would they be dead?

Sidney must have been thinking the same thing. He said, "Are Mommy and Daddy dead?"

"No."

I didn't know if it was true, but it was the right answer to give just then. That is, I hoped it was. What did I know?

Even if they felt the quake, if they weren't hurt, if they left right away, it would take more than an hour to drive home.

As I looked out over the canyon, I saw plumes of smoke rising into the brown cloud of dust that hung in the air. Smoke meant fires. Houses on fire.

I wondered if the fish felt the quake in the ocean. I wondered if there was going to be a tidal wave. Of course, living on a mountain, a tidal wave was the last thing I needed to worry about. Which didn't stop me from thinking about it.

"What do they say on the radio, Jennie?"

"They say the power's out all over the place. They're like: you should stay indoors. Then they're like: don't go into your house. They're trying to sound calm, but you can tell they're totally freaking out."

My mother had said that if we needed advice, we could call her sister, Aunt Annette, in Cupertino. But the phone was dead.

My mother had also said that if we needed to, we could go over to old Mr. Vanda's cabin. He'd be home. But Mr. Vanda's cabin had slid down the hill.

Oh my gosh.

Was he inside?

"Sidney. Jennie. We have to find Mr. Vanda. He may be hurt. He may be trapped in his house."

"First," Sidney said, "you have to find his house." I was surprised he could sound so sensible when he looked so scared. Did I sound sensible, too?

I moved as fast as I could with Sidney holding on to my pants pocket. With his other hand he carried the red parrot, which had a blue bandanna tied around its neck. Jennie followed, listening to her headphones.

"Tell me if you hear anything useful," I said.

She nodded. She said, "The Bay Bridge is closed. There's a hole in it. Some cars fell through."

So it wasn't just us. They'd felt it way up there, fifty miles away. Not just felt it — it had been strong enough to knock a hole in the Bay Bridge.

If it broke the Bay Bridge, what did it do to Candlestick Park?

My parents were dead. Jennie's mother, too. They were buried, crushed in the concrete rubble of what used to be a baseball stadium. I knew it for a certainty, felt it with a sudden tight, hard chill.

How would I tell Sidney? Would he make a joke? What would we do without parents? We'd be *orphans*.

I didn't stop what I was doing. I didn't give a sign that I knew they were dead. I was beginning to stop feeling. It seemed as if I were watching myself from a distance: There goes Franny. Her parents are dead. She's going to look for Mr. Vanda. There's her little brother carrying a parrot. There's her former best friend, blood drying on her chest, walking along with a bandage around her neck, listening to the radio.

Jennie said, "A freeway collapsed. In Oakland."

Oakland! Way over there!

Were all the roads closed? Even if my parents were alive, could they get home? Somehow, strangely, the thought gave me hope: They *could* be alive. My feelings weren't logical. I could observe them from a distance: There goes Franny. Her parents may not be dead after all. She's being irrational. She's upset. What can you expect? She's only a teenager.

In the road just beyond our house we came to a gap, a crack in the earth. Where there had been solid road, now there was a separation of about four feet with a ragged edge as if giant hands had ripped it apart. The crack was about six feet deep and went from one side of the road to the other, across the shoulder, and into the woods. We could smell the raw earth. Still, there wasn't a sound — not one birdcall, not one dog barking.

Again, Sidney seemed to read my mind. "Where's Lara?" he asked, staring into the pit.

If he could read my mind, I could read his. We were both staring into the gash in the earth, imagining a similar gash opening under Lara, swallowing her, closing and sealing her: buried alive.

"We've got to find Lara," Sidney said.

"Yes. After we find Mr. Vanda."

Maybe I could jump across the gap, but Sidney couldn't. We could climb down into the crack and then up the other side — but what if it closed? What if the same forces that had ripped the earth open came back and pushed it shut — with us inside?

We walked along the edge of the crack, following it into the woods. It became narrower just beyond the road, and a tree had fallen across the gap. We used the tree for a bridge. The forest almost overwhelmed me with the scent of fresh pine from all the trees and branches that had broken — a wonderful smell, usually, but now so powerful that it could have been a bathroom cleanser.

Mr. Vanda's mailbox still stood on a post by the road with the lettering on its side:

CHARLES VANDA
PHILOSOPHER
(RETIRED)

I once had asked Mr. Vanda how long he'd been retired, and he'd said he retired every night at ten o'clock and then unretired in the morning.

The rocks still smoked from where his propane tank had exploded, but the bush had burnt up without spreading the fire. The door to his chicken coop had flown open, and two hens were scurrying around with no idea where to go. All that remained of the cabin were some pier blocks and scattered pieces of lumber, twisted pipes sticking out of the ground, some firewood that had unstacked itself, and a Volkswagen lying on its side like a dead insect.

"Everything's like totally gnarfled," Jennie said.

"Yes," I said. I'd never heard the word *gnarfled* before, but I knew instantly what she meant. In the old days Jennie had always made up words — or grabbed them from television — and I'd always understood. I even knew how she'd spell it.

37

We headed downhill following the slide marks of the cabin. It was easy to track. Through what had been a carpet of wildflowers the house had gouged the ground like a glacier, leaving rocks and raw dirt. The hillside was so steep that we had to hang on to roots and the broken bottoms of bushes — the house had sliced off the tops.

Where the ground leveled off, there was the cabin — only it wasn't a cabin anymore but a messy pile of lumber.

"Mr. Vanda?" I called. "Are you there? Can you hear me?"

No answer.

Again a strange detachment settled over me. I climbed over two-by-fours — and watched myself from a distance — lifting handfuls of roofing shingles, throwing them to the side, cutting my fingers on rusty nails, calling over and over: "Mr. Vanda! Can you hear me?"

And then we heard something: a voice, Mr. Vanda's voice, sounding weak and far away as if he was buried way at the bottom of the pile.

We heard it again.

"He's up there," Sidney said, pointing uphill.

We scrambled up the hillside, which was much harder than going down, slipping, rocks giving way under our feet, grasping at broken stalks.

Back where the cabin had been, I still didn't see him. Then something groaned. Some clothing was sticking out from under the car. I ran to the drive-way and found that the clothing was Mr. Vanda, sprawled on his back on the ground under the car with blood oozing out of his forehead, eyes shut. His head was turned sideways with the side vent window resting on it.

"He's dead," Sidney said, and he hugged the red parrot.

"I ain't," Mr. Vanda said, and he opened his eyes.

"Are you stuck?" Sidney asked.

"I'm sort of . . . inconvenienced."

Now my detachment was complete. I heard my-self tell Jennie and Sidney to help. I watched us as we kneeled next to the car, put our hands under the rain gutter at the side of the roof — and lifted.

We straightened our backs and lifted, and rose off our knees and kept lifting, and shifted our weight as the car arched backwards from us and kept lifting, and then the car took on a life of its own and fell back from our hands and thumped upright.

Mr. Vanda didn't move.

We lifted a Volkswagen. I can't say that we did it so much as I saw us doing it. The thumping of the

Volkswagen seemed to jar me back into my head. My hands were shaking; my fingers were sore. I couldn't believe what we had done.

Mr. Vanda was wincing.

"We'll help you get up," I said.

"Don't," he said, not moving his head.

"What's the matter?"

"Something's broke. Hip. Leg. Something."

"What happened?"

"I was washing dishes. First thing I knew, the water came up out of the sink and splashed me in the face. Next thing I knew, I was flying through the window."

"Was it open?" Sidney asked.

"I opened it," Mr. Vanda said. "The hard way."

"Are you okay?" Sidney asked.

I couldn't believe it. The man had been thrown through his kitchen window, his face was bleeding, a car had fallen on him, his leg or hip or something was broken, his house had disappeared, he was probably in incredible pain, and Sidney wanted to know if he was okay.

Mr. Vanda looked at Sidney clutching the red parrot with a grip that would strangle a real animal, and he must have known what Sidney needed.

"Yeah." Mr. Vanda closed his eyes. "I'm okay."

40

Sidney loosened his grip slightly on the parrot. "We found your house, Mr. Vanda," he said.

"Thank you, Sidney," Mr. Vanda said. He grimaced. He *was* in pain. His eyes were still closed. "Get help," he said.

I wished I knew what to do for Mr. Vanda's bleeding head and broken body. I wished my father were here. He wasn't a medic anymore — he worked for a biotech company — but still, he'd know exactly what to do.

Jennie kneeled down next to Mr. Vanda. "We need to stop his bleeding," she said. "I need a bandage. A clean cloth. Something. The parrot's bandanna. Sid. Give me Squawk."

Without a word, Sid handed the red parrot to Jennie. Not his normal behavior, doing what was asked. But today was not a normal day.

Jennie folded the bandanna and pressed it over the cut. She seemed to be taking care not to let any blood come in contact with her body. "Does that hurt?"

"Naw."

"Can you hold it there? Keep the pressure on? It'll stop the bleeding."

"Okay." Mr. Vanda put his hand on the bandanna.

Thank you, Jennie. You can visit me anytime we have an earthquake. While I stand around in confusion, you know exactly what to do. And calmly, coolly, you do it.

Mr. Vanda's body shivered. It was a hot day, but he was lying on the ground, and evening was coming.

"You need a blanket," I said.

"I'll find one," Sidney said.

He ran — and slipped — and tumbled down the hill toward the remains of the house. I didn't think he could find anything in that wreck. I couldn't have found a bed, much less a blanket. In a minute, though, Sidney came climbing back dragging a yellow window curtain. We shook it out and spread it over the old man.

"We'll get help," I said.

"Do that," Mr. Vanda said.

"Can we make you more comfortable?"

"No."

"Will you be all right?"

Mr. Vanda closed his eyes. "I'll have to be," he said.

GWEN

We hurried down the road. Sidney no longer held on to my blue jeans, but he stayed right by my side, smothering Squawk in a bear hug to his chest with both arms.

"What's happening?" I asked Jennie.

"Big fires in San Francisco. In the Marina. Some apartments collapsed."

"Anything about Candlestick Park?"

"No." There was a catch in her voice. "I'll try a different station."

For just a moment, I met Jennie's eyes. Without a word I knew that she was just as worried about her mother as I was about my parents. And in that moment I noticed how good it felt that Jennie and I could still communicate eye to eye, without speaking.

"Anything about what's happening around here?"

"No. Nothing."

I wondered whether the shaking on our mountain had been too insignificant to be reported on the radio. Or whether they simply didn't know about us. Or didn't care.

"We've got to find Lara," Sidney said. "Maybe a car fell on her."

"First," I said, "we've got to find help for Mr. Vanda."

Normally when you have an emergency on the mountain, you call the volunteer fire department. Normally, you have a working phone. In a working house.

We moved on up the road — not quite running, but faster than walking — to a big house, a new one. It didn't look particularly damaged except for a brick chimney that had broken off at the roofline and spilled its bricks down the shingles to the gutter. Some windows had cracked. A Winnebago was parked in the driveway. It didn't seem to be damaged, either.

I wondered how one house could fly completely apart while another one nearby seemed scarcely touched. Mr. Vanda's chicken coop still stood. The old shed down below my house seemed unharmed. How were they different?

The front door was open — probably from the quake. I went to it and knocked.

No one answered.

Books and magazines and knickknacks were scattered all over the floor. I saw a telephone.

"Hey!" I called. "Anybody home?"

I went inside. It was eerie, going into somebody's house. I felt guilty somehow. Like a burglar. I tried the phone. Dead. Probably every line on the mountain was down. We'd have to go to the firehouse, about a mile.

Coming out, I saw that the propane tank downhill from the house was upright but lopsided.

Did I really want to mess with another propane tank? It seemed, before I'd even finished thinking up the question, that I was on my way down.

"Where are you going?" Sidney shouted.

"To shut off their propane."

"Franny, be careful," Jennie called.

The pipe was still connected to the tank, but I smelled gas. Which didn't tell me anything because by now the whole mountain seemed to smell of gas. I reached for the handle, and then a thought struck me: What if an aftershock happened right now? What if this tank rolled off and carried you with it? What if it blew? Why are you doing this? Nobody's life is in danger — except yours.

I couldn't answer the questions, but I turned the handle until it was tightly shut. Then I ran.

I couldn't bear the thought of another tank blowing up, another fire, another possibility of setting the whole hillside aflame. Maybe that's why I did it. Maybe not.

We hurried on. Houses are not side by side on Loma Prieta. Sometimes they're a good distance apart. I saw three horses in a pasture, skittish, wild-eyed.

At the next two houses we passed, propane tanks were standing at various odd angles. Each time, I ran to them and shut them off.

"Franny, you're brave," Jennie said.

"Or stupid," I said.

"Right," Sid said.

The next house that we passed had slid in one piece off its foundation and was now leaning against a redwood tree. Flames were roaring out of two windows. A woman was standing near the flames, cursing the garden hose in her hand. Two small children sat at a picnic table in the yard, looking terrified. A few drops of water dribbled from the hose.

I called to the woman: "Is anybody inside the house?"

"No," she shouted back. "Could you run to the fire station?"

"We're on our way."

Now I really ran. Jennie ran. Sidney ran behind me, choking the red parrot, begging me to slow down. I let him catch up, then ran at an easier pace. Too many people were depending on me. Sidney needed me. Mr. Vanda needed help. Lara might be trapped somewhere. And now a woman's house was on fire with no way to call the volunteer fire department. We ran past a house that had cracked in half, like an egg. With each new wreck of a home that I encountered, I felt a sickening tug in my chest. Everywhere the air reeked of gas. One propane tank had actually bounced into the branches of a tree and hung there like a beached whale.

This was Hell. This was the world I'd grown up in, the world I lived in, my home — now fallen and twisted and shaken apart.

How many houses were on fire right now? How many houses had nobody home to stop the flames? How many had no fire extinguisher? How many had broken waterlines? How many had collapsed?

I saw a man running ahead of us in the same direction. We passed telephone poles leaning at odd angles with wires draping down. The big black transformers had dropped off the poles and crashed to the ground. They had a smell like a burned-out motor.

Then we shook again. Another aftershock. I almost lost my balance but managed to stay on my feet. Another BOOM from far away made me wince. The pavement of the street cracked open right in front of my eyes. It wasn't a deep crack and only a couple of inches wide. We just stepped over it. Sidney's fingers went back to clenching my belt loop. The red parrot he carried in his armpit.

We came to the firehouse. The doors were open; one truck was gone. A man — the same man who I'd seen running ahead of me — was listening to the CB radio in another truck and jotting something down on a pad of yellow paper. He looked up at me. He was bald but had a full mustache and beard. With amazement he said, "There are at least eleven houses on fire."

I told him about the house that was leaning against a redwood tree with the woman cursing her garden hose.

"Make that twelve," he said. He grabbed an extinguisher and started running down the road.

"Don't you want to take the truck?" I called after him.

"It's broken," he shouted as he kept on running. A big key ring attached to his belt went jangling behind him, bouncing on his butt.

An extinguisher wouldn't be enough to save that house.

I hadn't had a chance to tell him about Mr. Vanda.

On the ground in front of the firehouse I saw a dead ground squirrel. What had killed it? I thought of all the animals that lived underground. Their tunnels had probably collapsed. How many would die? How many were buried alive? How many were desperately digging at this very moment, digging for their lives?

Where was Lara?

A black Chevy camper truck came roaring down the narrow road and screeched to a stop in front of the firehouse. A woman with wet hair jumped out and looked around. "Are they all *gone*?" she asked.

"There are twelve houses on fire," I said.

"And we've got what? Two trucks? Half a dozen volunteers?"

"Did you come to report a fire?" I asked.

"I came to see if I could *help*."

"You could help me." I told her about Mr. Vanda.

"Get in," she said, and she climbed into the cab of the camper truck. Sidney, Jennie, and I crammed in beside her. "I'm a nurse," she said as she backed out. "My name's Gwen. Excuse the hair. I was in the shower when it happened. It threw me right out the door." She had the radio on. I heard — as Jennie had said — that the Marina District of San Francisco was on fire. A section had fallen out of the Bay Bridge. A freeway had collapsed in Oakland. People were trapped. People had died — maybe hundreds. Maybe thousands.

Then I heard the announcement: The World Series game had been postponed indefinitely. They said that the power was out at Candlestick Park, a few people had been taken to the hospital, and they didn't know if the structure was safe though, it definitely had not fallen down.

They were *alive.*

My parents — and Jennie's mother — couldn't be among those few people who had been taken to the hospital. I knew it for a fact, just as a few minutes ago I had known that they were dead.

I felt flooded with relief and yet overcome with worry at the same time. I needed them to come home. I wanted them to tell me what to do. I wanted them to hold my hand and say don't be scared and tell me everything would be all right.

But of course, everything *wasn't* all right.

Sidney was looking up at me. "What's gonna happen now?" he asked.

"We're going to help Mr. Vanda. Gwen's a nurse."

"Then we'll find Lara?"

"We'll try."

"Then what'll we do?"

"Don't worry." I patted his hand. "We'll be all right."

Gwen drove fast — too fast. She bounced right over the cracks in the road. I wondered if she would try to jump the truck over the big gap separating the pavement not far from my house, but she didn't need to. Mr. Vanda's house — that is, ex-house — was on the near side.

We passed the house that had been burning out of two windows. The fire had now spread across the entire side. The woman was at a safe distance standing by the road, holding her two children, watching it burn.

Gwen stopped.

I called out the truck window: "Did a man come here?"

The woman nodded her head in the direction of an extinguisher that lay on the ground, empty and abandoned.

"He's gone already?"

The woman nodded again. "He went to look for people who might be trapped or hurt. He said they had to let houses burn. He said they had to help people first."

She seemed weary and hopeless. But of course the fireman was right.

Except for the redwood tree that the house was leaning against, there was a clearing around the building. Most people had learned the lesson of the previous wildfire and kept a firebreak around their houses. It had rained recently, so things weren't tinder dry. There was no wind. This fire, at least, wouldn't spread. I hoped the tree would survive. Redwoods usually manage to slough off flames with their tough bark. And they're full of water. They're like giant wooden water tanks.

Maybe it was silly of me to be worrying about the life of a redwood in the middle of all this destruction. But I did. I care about redwoods. Those trees were full-grown before I was ever born, and they'll be around long after I'm gone. These same trees will — with luck — still be alive in the year 3000. Think of that.

Gwen drove on.

She parked next to Mr. Vanda's Volkswagen. She left the door open and the radio on.

We had *lifted* that Volkswagen.

The yellow window curtain was now pulled up over Mr. Vanda's face. Something slipped in my gut. *Oh, no*, I thought. *He's dead.* But as we walked toward him, he flipped the curtain down to his shoulders.

He was no longer holding the bandanna to his forehead. The bleeding had stopped; the blood was drying where it had trickled down toward his ear. As soon as he exposed his face, a couple of flies started pestering him. He shooed them with his hand — and I understood why he'd covered himself.

"Are you comfortable?" Gwen asked.

"Bored," Mr. Vanda said. "Pain is very boring."

"Where does it hurt?"

"Here." Mr. Vanda touched his hip.

Gwen touched him lightly. "Here?"

"Yes."

"What about here?"

"Yes."

"And here?"

Wincing. "Yes."

Gwen turned to Jennie and me — and to Sidney, who was latched to my jeans with one hand and squeezing the parrot with the other. "We can't call an ambulance," she said. "I'll take him to the hospital. We'll all have to work together to move him." She went to the camper truck and lifted a mattress from the back, then removed a bed board that was underneath it. She explained to us that the idea would be to move Mr. Vanda as little as possible in transferring him to the bed board. Gwen would place her hands on either side of the hip; I was to lift his shoulders; Sid, his head; Jennie, his legs. We would "logroll" him, she called it, keeping him stiff as a log while rolling him to his side, sliding the bed board under, then rolling him back onto it.

Sidney set the parrot on the ground.

"On three," Gwen said. "One. Two. Three."

After lifting a Volkswagen, rolling Mr. Vanda was no problem at all.

"Oof," Mr. Vanda grunted.

"Hurt?" Gwen asked.

"Not bad," Mr. Vanda said.

Gwen and Sidney took one end, Jennie and I the other, and we carried Mr. Vanda on the bed board to the back of the truck. Then Sid ran back for Squawk and gently tucked him next to Mr. Vanda's head.

It was, for Sidney, a major act of kindness. Mr. Vanda smiled at Sidney and closed his eyes.

Gwen closed Mr. Vanda up in the rear.

The radio was still on. They were talking about Highway 17. Our highway, the road to our mountain, was closed due to landslides triggered by the earthquake.

If it was closed, Gwen couldn't take Mr. Vanda to a hospital. And my parents couldn't come home.

Now I really felt alone. My parents weren't dead, but if they couldn't get here, I was just as alone. I felt like an orphan.

"Where will you take him?" I asked Gwen.

"To the school, I guess."

"If it's still there," I said.

The school was the community center. The gymnasium was a multipurpose room with a kitchen and a stage. All kinds of meetings and events were held there. This afternoon, in fact, they had been setting up for a volleyball tournament.

The school was supposed to be emergency headquarters in a disaster.

Of course, I thought. This is it. This is a *disaster*.

"Good luck," I said to Gwen.

Now, at last, we had time to look for Lara.

ERIC

We went back to the house to see if Lara had come home. Nothing had changed except that the sun was lower in the sky. The propane tank still lay on its side. The old stone chimney still lay on the ground, as did the water heater. Broken glass was everywhere. Bloodstains made a trail across the floor, leading to the doorway from the window where Jennie had been standing.

And no sign of Lara.

I said, "If we split up and spread out, we have a better chance of finding her."

Sidney's face looked troubled. So, as a matter of fact, did Jennie's. "Let's like — stick together," she said. "Okay?"

Actually, I didn't like the idea of splitting up, either.

"Where shall we look?" Jennie asked.

I'd last seen her heading toward the road. I could think of nothing better than to go that way. Which way? We'd already gone to the firehouse without seeing her, though we hadn't made a thorough search. So now I figured we should go the opposite way.

We wandered down the narrow country road. It was the same route I used to take with Lara every day, which seemed ever so long ago — before today. I'd always loved the walk. The roadside was a riot of wildflowers: orange poppy, yellow mustard, purple vetch, daisies, yarrow, wild rose. A goldfinch darted in and out among blackberry branches. Beyond a split-rail fence lay a rolling field of dry oat grass that would whisper and crackle in the wind. Here and there among the golden oats stood a spot of dark green: a live-oak tree, solitary, craggy, and cool.

We called Lara's name. I whistled with my fingers against my teeth — something I learned from my mother. My father and Sidney couldn't whistle like that, and it had always made them jealous.

Sidney tried, but all that came out was drool.

"What if she's buried?" Sidney asked. "How will we know she's there?"

"She isn't buried," I said.

"How do you know?"

"If she's smart enough to run out of the house before there's an earthquake, she's smart enough to find a safe place to stay."

"How do you know?"

"Instink," I said.

But I wasn't as sure as I sounded. I had visions of Lara trapped under a fallen tree or squashed by a boulder or incinerated by an exploding propane tank — and so, I knew, did Sidney. Sidney, who loved violence. Sidney, who in spite of the occasional joke, was obviously scared to death. It was for his sake that I was trying to appear calm and confident. Meanwhile another part of my mind was telling me that I was a phony. A fake. If I was honest, if I was true to my feelings, I'd cry and scream and generally lose control. But what would that accomplish?

I asked Jennie, "What do you hear?"

"Gridlock on the freeways," she said. "If they're coming, it'll take hours."

"The road's closed, Jennie."

"I know."

"It can take days to clear a landslide. Weeks, even."

"I know."

Jennie walked right beside me, shoulder to shoulder. On the other side Sidney held one finger through a belt loop of my Levi's. I felt as close to Jennie — not just physically, but in terms of friendship, of trust, of sharing — as in the good old days when we were friends. Which we still were, I now saw. At the same time I felt a new bond with Sidney. The earthquake had shaken more than just earth and houses and roads. More than just *things*.

We came to a house where several cars had

parked carelessly, blocking the entire road, and a commotion of people had gathered in the front yard. The man from the firehouse — the bald man with the full mustache and beard — was kneeling over a body on the ground, surrounded by stones. A man beside him was cutting strips of gauze, and a woman was readying a stretcher. Watching from a few feet away was Mrs. Gunderson, whose house it was, holding her little daughter Katie in her arms, wrapped tight. Katie, like any wiggly four-year-old, looked as if she wanted to get away. Mrs. Gunderson seemed upset. She looked as if she wasn't going to let go of Katie for a long, long time.

"Can we help?" Jennie asked.

"Is he dead?" Sidney asked.

"He's alive," Mrs. Gunderson said. "And he's in good hands. Thank you, though."

Now I recognized that body on the ground. "It's Billy!"

Billy was a stonemason. He wasn't the brightest guy in the world, but he was friendly, and he sure knew how to lay stones. He had long scraggly hair, a beard that hung to his chest, and looked like the old man of the mountain — though he wasn't that old. His trademark was a swirling, circular pattern that he somehow managed to build into every wall and chimney and barbecue that he worked on.

He'd built the chimney on our cabin, which was now a heap of rubble just like what was on the ground here.

"He was building a wall," Mrs. Gunderson said. "It was beautiful. Nearly done. Katie was asking questions. You know how she is. Pestering him, but of course Billy didn't mind. She was standing right against the wall when it started to shake. Billy grabbed her — in an instant — never hesitated — and fell down on top of her. He shielded her with his body. He saved her life. The whole wall fell on top of them. I was freaked out. When we dug them out, Katie didn't have a scratch."

Billy had more than a scratch. He was unconscious. They were moving him to the stretcher.

Mrs. Gunderson looked at Billy, then back at us, and said, "How do you *thank* somebody for doing something like that?"

We couldn't answer. If Sidney and I were in a similar situation, if there was no time for thinking and I was acting purely on instinct, would I fall on Sid and shield him with my body?

I asked Mrs. Gunderson if she'd seen Lara.

"No. But I've been kind of distracted."

They put Billy in the back of a Volvo station wagon with its seats folded down. Sidney stared at the bandages wrapped round Billy's head. He didn't say a word. He held tight to my belt loop.

I asked, "Where will you take him?"

"To the school." The bald man with the mustache and beard looked us over. "Are you guys all right?"

We must have been a sight. We were smudged all over with dirt from scrambling up and down Mr. Vanda's hillside. I'd gotten some white powder in my hair from the fire extinguisher. Sidney had brushed against some scorched rock, too, giving him a black arm. And Jennie had a bandage around her neck and dried blood all over her shirt.

"We're fine," I said.

We walked on.

Soon we came to Eric's house. Even from a distance I could see cracks and jagged gray holes in the stucco siding. The chimney had broken off at the top. Most of the windows were broken. An old concrete gatepost had gnarfled into the driveway.

Just as if nothing unusual had occurred today, the front door opened and Eric "just happened" to come out as I was walking by.

"Oh. Hi, Franny," Eric called across the yard. "I was just coming out to see if the newspaper had been delivered."

I stopped walking. Jennie and Sidney stopped

beside me. Eric walked toward us up the driveway. He stepped over the fallen gatepost without a second glance and said what he always said: "What's new?"

Suddenly I laughed. It surprised me, but it felt wonderful.

"Oh, nothing much," I said. "What's new with you?"

"Oh, you know." He shrugged. "Nothing ever happens around here."

"Eric, this is Sidney. And this is my old friend, Jennie."

"Hey, Sidney. I've heard a lot about you. Hey, Jennie."

Sidney didn't say anything. Which didn't surprise me. Normally he would stick out his tongue — or worse — in a situation like this. But Jennie didn't say anything, either. Which did surprise me. She looked annoyed.

"So what've you been doing?" I asked.

"Nothing special. I was just shoveling out the bathroom."

"Shoveling?"

"All the tile fell out of the shower."

I asked Eric where he had been when it happened. He said he'd just sat down to watch the pregame show for the World Series when the screen went blank. Suddenly books were flying at him and bricks were thundering down outside the window. For a moment he'd thought it must be raining bricks — like you hear people say it's raining cats and dogs — and then he realized that the chimney was falling down.

Jennie was looking more annoyed.

I started to tell Eric what had happened at our house.

"Franny . . ." Jennie said impatiently.

"All right," I said. Maybe it was rude of me to hold a private conversation — but she could have joined in.

"Have you seen Lara?" I asked.

"Sure. About a half hour ago. I was just happening to come out to — I don't know — to take out some garbage. But Lara was by herself. Just trotting along. What's up, Franny? Are you and your dog taking separate walks now? Did you have a quarrel?"

Jennie was looking annoyed again.

"Lara's lost," I said.

"Actually," Eric said, "I think Lara probably knows exactly where she is. She's not lost. It's just that you guys can't find her."

Jennie was not amused. "Which way did she go?"

Eric pointed down the road in the direction we had been heading.

"Let's go," Jennie said.

"Can I help you look?" Eric asked.

"Sure," I said.

"No," Jennie said. Now she looked uncomfortable, as if she knew she was acting strangely. "I mean, don't come with us. Look somewhere else. And if you see her" — Jennie fished in her pocket and pulled out some M&M's — "give her these."

"I can't do that," Eric said. "I wouldn't want to hurt her."

"I didn't say to *kick* her," Jennie said. "I said to give her an M&M."

Eric frowned. "Don't you know chocolate is bad for dogs?"

"Uh — what?" Jennie looked as if she were the one who'd been kicked.

"It makes them sick," Eric said. "There's something in the cocoa bean. It's poison to them."

Jennie looked stricken. The only other time I'd seen that look on her face was after she'd accidentally dropped a hamster and broken its leg. In a very small voice she said, "How do you know?"

"A friend of mine," Eric said. "His mother had a little Pekingese that ripped into some See's candy. Ate half the box. It died. The vet said it was too much chocolate for such a little dog. They'd always given her candy. She loved the stuff. But half a box was too much. At least, my friend figured, the dog died happy."

Jennie's voice was strained: "Come on, Franny." She started walking.

I nodded a good-bye to Eric and followed Jennie down the road.

Sidney tugged on my belt loop. "Is Lara alive?"

"She has to be," I said. "Eric saw her, and she didn't have time to run all the way to his house before the quake, so she must have made it through okay."

"Why didn't she come home?"

"She must be spooked."

"Or poisoned," Jennie said.

"Oh, come on, Jennie. One peanut butter cup isn't going to kill her. You used to give her lots more chocolate than that when she was only a little puppy."

"How *could* I?"

"You didn't know."

"How could I not know? How could I be so — so *ignorant*? So *stupid*?"

"You aren't stupid. I bet lots of people don't know that chocolate is bad for dogs. I didn't know."

"Of *all* the people to learn it from. That little . . . *jerk*!"

"He's not a jerk, Jennie."

"Of course *you'd* say that." Jennie stared straight ahead. She wouldn't look at me. "How could you, Franny?"

"How could I what?"

"Oh, come on."

"What?"

"Cut the crap."

"What are you talking about?"

"Anybody can see that he's crazy about you."

"I wouldn't say that. Not exactly."

"And you're crazy about him."

"I am not. Well. You know. I like him. But I hardly know him. The only time I ever see him outside of school is when I happen to walk the dog by his — "

"Cut the crap."

"Jennie, stop *saying* that. What's bothering you?"

"Nothing."

"Don't you want to talk about it?"

Jennie didn't answer. Suddenly, it seemed, her headphones didn't allow her to hear my voice.

This, I reflected, was the old Jennie, too. Jennie the dramatic. Jennie the volcano. And when she was mad at me — sometimes with good reason, sometimes not — she wouldn't talk about it for days.

We had been walking through a section of forest where the road dipped down and crossed a creek on a bridge of wooden planks. The water, I saw, was running fuller and faster than it had the day before even though there had been no rain in that time. Had water shaken out of the earth?

Lara always stopped for a drink here. I paused, whistled, called her name. The gurgle of water was the only reply.

Up a short hill and around a bend we came out of the trees to where — until now — a white barn in a pasture overlooked a vista of the mountainside. The barn had collapsed. The walls had splayed out, and the triangle of roof and hayloft had crashed straight down.

Jennie looked frantic. "Do you think there're *animals* in there?"

No other people were in sight. Where was the farmer? Before I could say anything, Jennie had let herself through the barbed wire fence and was running to the barn.

I glanced around the pasture. Sometimes a bull grazed there. Today there were only cows, udders bulging. I wondered if the farmer had gone to town and couldn't get back because the road was closed. Or had his house fallen in on him? No, it stood. Or the barn?

"Follow me, Sid."

We let ourselves through the fence and ran after Jennie. She was on her hands and knees, peering under the bottom of the hayloft, which stood about two feet above the floor of the barn, held up by the debris of the fallen walls. You could see through the darkness clear to daylight on the other end.

"The cows were all out in the pasture," I said.

Then we heard a mournful, blatting sound.

Jennie ran around to the side of the barn. Sid and I followed. Jennie was cooing soothing words and rubbing her hands over the side of a goat that had soulful eyes and an orange tag attached to its ear. It was standing on three legs. The fourth was broken, dangling at a sickening angle. The sight made me gag. I'd never make a good doctor. Or vet.

"Careful, Jennie," I said. "If he's hurt, he might do anything. He might bite you."

"Poor, poor, little goat," Jennie was cooing. "You need to lie down. I'll get you some straw."

With a ferocious look in her eye, Jennie grabbed a bale of straw that the barn had crushed, and she ripped it open with her bare hands. She spread out

68

a bed and then gently pulled at the goat, cooing, kissing the scrubby fur of its neck, and actually got it to drop awkwardly onto the straw.

From her pocket Jennie produced a couple of dirty M&M's, stared at them a moment, then offered them to the grateful animal. "Goats can eat anything, right?"

She turned away, a tear on her cheek.

I didn't say anything. I didn't have high hopes for that beast. What's a farmer going to do to a goat with a broken leg?

As we crossed the pasture and returned to the road, I wondered what would happen to the cows if the farmer couldn't get home to milk them. Could I help? I'd never milked a cow.

Stop, Franny, I told myself. You can't help everything.

But I worried about them.

I knew without asking what Sidney was thinking as he walked along attached to my belt loop. He had visions of Lara with a broken leg.

So did I.

THE SCHOOL

We hadn't found Lara even though we had walked all the way to Summit Road, which ran along the top of our mountain ridge. Just as we got there, a woman with a haunted look went zooming past us in a Jeep Cherokee going way too fast. She scared me.

She must be hurrying home to her kids, I thought. I hope she doesn't kill anybody on the way.

Without discussion, without even thinking about where we were going, I started down Summit Road. Our shadows were long.

In ten minutes, staying far to the side whenever a car came (usually too fast) (was everybody crazy?) (what if Lara got hit by a car?), we arrived at the school.

As we entered the driveway, we passed the big sign that said GO CHEETAHS. Once again, a sense of detachment settled over me. Though I spent six hours a day at this place, I felt as if I were seeing it for the first time. I looked around. Dropping away from the schoolyard on three sides was a Christmas tree farm, over which you could see mountains and misty canyons, pine forest, orchards, scattered houses — and five plumes of smoke. Five houses on fire.

The school buildings were still standing. Gutters and downspouts had detached from the roof and hung freely in the air. There were cracks in the sidewalks. Swallows had built dozens of mud nests under the eaves of the roof, and now all the nests had shaken loose and fallen like dry mud bombs onto the concrete passageway. The swallows were swooping and calling with no home to return to.

Usually from the school grounds you could hear the distant muffled roar of traffic on the freeway, Highway 17, three miles away. Now it was silent. The highway was closed.

This school where I had spent so much time seemed oddly familiar and yet not quite real, like a dream. I felt suddenly so much older than just a few hours ago. Things like the GO CHEETAHS sign — who cares whether the volleyball team wins or loses? My homework assignments for the night — I couldn't even remember what they were. What did they matter? Posters announcing a Halloween Hop — kid stuff. A crack had opened in my life and I was now a different person returning to visit a school that I had attended long ago. I could be on the far side of twenty-one. I wasn't just a teenager anymore.

Groups of people were standing and sitting in clumps scattered on the grass of the playing fields. There were two groups of boys, sixth-, seventh-, eighth-graders, who were the two visiting teams that had come for the volleyball tournament. Now the tournament had stopped, and they couldn't go home. They couldn't even phone home to find out if they still had houses to return to.

Someone had carried bright blue gymnastics mats out of the multipurpose room and laid them on the baseball diamond. Lying on the mats were about a dozen injured people, tended by a woman. Gwen. I had been wandering about in something of a daze, but when Jennie spotted the injured people on the mats, she headed right toward them. I followed, and Sidney of course followed me. Gwen, wearing rubber gloves, was tending to a woman who'd been cut all over — by flying glass, I'll bet — and was bleeding on to the mat. My stomach turned. Gwen's hair had dried unbrushed.

"Can I help?" Jennie asked.

Gwen nodded toward a first aid box lying open beside her. "Put on these gloves." She was busy tying some gauze.

Jennie slipped the gloves on, took some scissors from Gwen's lap, and snipped where Gwen was holding the gauze. A team had formed. I couldn't help. I just didn't have the constitution for it. Beside the bleeding woman lay a man with a broken arm that was pointing out from his body; beside him lay Billy mummified in gauze, unconscious. On another mat, Gwen explained to Jennie, was a pregnant woman who was in premature labor. Then the corner of my eye caught an unmistakable red parrot. To the side, peacefully staring up at nothing in particular, lay Mr. Vanda.

Him I could handle.

I stood looming over him so that Sidney and I were blocking his view of the sky. "Anything I can do for you?" I asked.

"No, I'm quite comfortable," he said. "As long as I don't move."

Sidney tucked Squawk back where he thought he belonged, next to Mr. Vanda's head.

"Thanks, Sid," Mr. Vanda said, and he closed his eyelids. A moment later he opened them again. He was gazing right into my eyes. "You're heroes," he said.

"I don't know what I'm doing," I said.

"That's the best kind of hero," he said. "Unrehearsed. Fumbling. An everyday sort. A small hero. Bless you all."

I accepted his blessing. A sweet feeling came over me. I had been running on adrenaline and reflexes

73

for the last hour or so, reacting rather than planning, doing rather than thinking. If we were heroes, we were definitely the everyday sort. Coping. Improvising. Small.

Sid was staring at the other people on the mats with a particularly long look at the man with the broken arm that seemed to have two elbows working in opposite directions. Sid didn't say a word.

"Sidney!"

He looked up. It was Mrs. LaFeau, his teacher, the one he called Mrs. Lipo.

"Sidney! It's so good to see that you're all right. I'm so *worried* about everybody."

Normally when somebody said something like that, Sidney would burp or do something equally rude, but right then he looked absolutely numb. What he did was walk straight to Mrs. LaFeau. She leaned down, opened her arms, and hugged Sid up against her enormous bosom. Sid offered no resistance.

"Where were you when it happened?" Mrs. LaFeau asked.

"Outside our house," Sidney answered.

"The *best* place to be," Mrs. LaFeau said, releasing him from her jiggling arms. "Outside. Where nothing can fall on you."

"Trees were falling," Sid said. "And *boulders*. And apples."

"That must have been scary."

"It *was*."

I had never heard Sid admit that anything was scary before.

"I was in the classroom, all alone," Mrs. LaFeau said. "Suddenly the ceiling tiles started falling, and the lights started swinging, and all the drawers shot out of the filing cabinet, and the bookshelf dropped all the books on the floor. I crawled under the desk, but I didn't *fit*. And then the desk walked away from me. When it was over, the door was jammed shut. I had to climb out a window."

I would have giggled, imagining big old Mrs. LaFeau climbing out the classroom window or, even better, trying to fit herself under a desk, but at the time nothing was funny. Later, remembering, we all smiled.

"Where are your parents?" Mrs. LaFeau asked.

Sidney explained that they had gone to the World Series.

"Would you like to stay with me right now?" Mrs. LaFeau asked, and she held out her pudgy pale hand.

Immediately, Sid took it — latched on to it as he

had latched on to my blue jeans. I saw that Mrs. LaFeau had several other children with her. I knew those kids. They went to child care after school. Now, like Sid and me, they were earthquake orphans until their parents could find a way home.

I looked back at the mats. Jennie, still in her headphones, kneeled by the woman in labor, held her hand, and started talking to her. I didn't see any medical supplies except the white metal first aid box that I recognized as the one that normally hung on the wall in the hallway by the principal's office. Gwen was talking about triage, which meant sorting people out according to how they were hurt.

So Sid was latched to Mrs. LaFeau. Jennie was occupied. And I . . .

I was free!

I still didn't have my mother and father. I didn't know where my dog had run to or if she was okay. I didn't know whether my house was going to fall down. But at least at this moment in this place surrounded by people helping people, I felt safe. And nobody was hanging on to my belt loop.

I looked around. The sun was a flat orange blob sinking into the ocean. The last shafts of light swirled with smoke and dust.

In those first moments of freedom I suddenly

realized that I was hungry. Before I could do anything, however, Mr. Perkins came storming toward me. Mr. Perkins was a wiry little man with a thin bony face and wild bushy black hair that looked like a bird's nest. He looked like a short Bill Cosby wearing a wig. We called him the mad scientist, but he was my favorite teacher.

"Frances!" he barked. "Don't just stand there. Come with me."

I fell in step beside him. He was walking, but I had to jog to keep up.

"What do you want?" I asked.

"We have to find out why there isn't any water."

I followed his strides across the road and through the maintenance yard where they park the school buses. We could hear running water though there was no creek there. Soon we saw why: The big green water storage tank had cracked a seam. All the water was gushing out and gurgling down a ravine.

"There goes a hundred thousand gallons," Mr. Perkins said. "That was supposed to be our emergency supply."

"Where does it come from?" I asked.

"Good question." Mr. Perkins looked at me approvingly. He'd always liked me. And I liked him. I liked school. I was actually glad that the school buildings hadn't fallen down. "It comes from a well," Mr. Perkins explained. "The only way to get water out of the well is with the pump. The *electric* pump." He looked across the road to the school and the orange, twilit sky. "There won't be power for days."

Suddenly he was walking again, and I was jogging to keep up with him.

"Still making earrings, Frances? Still have a collection of pretty little stones?"

"I . . . don't know. It was in the house."

"Did you lose your house?"

"No. But it shook pretty badly."

"I guess some new rocks got formed today. Or at least got pulverized. Just think, Frances. We are taking part in a geologic *event*. What a *privilege*."

Somehow I didn't feel privileged. Mr. Perkins, I decided, may be a good teacher but he's also slightly *demented*. All I said was: "I like it better when I just come along afterward and collect the rocks."

Back at the school Sidney was still clinging to Mrs. LaFeau's hand and Jennie was still helping Gwen with first aid. There were now fifteen bodies on the mats. Somebody was covering them with blankets loaned by neighbors from the houses nearby. There was a handmade afghan. And a com-

78

forter with bright printed trucks on it that had obviously come from some child's bed.

I stayed with Mr. Perkins. A woman with two children came up to him and asked where the bathroom was. Mr. Perkins pointed to the Christmas tree farm. "Pick a tree," he said.

I needed to go, too, but not that badly. Not yet.

"Where's the police?" the woman asked. "Where's the ambulance? Where's the Red Cross?"

"Help is on the way," Mr. Perkins said.

"When?"

"Soon."

The woman seemed reassured. She headed with her two children toward the Christmas tree farm.

"What help is coming, Mr. Perkins?" I asked.

He shrugged. "I have no idea. We have no contact with the rest of the world. They don't even know if we have a problem here. They can't *drive* here. They can't *phone* here."

"Then why'd you tell her help is on the way? And *soon*."

"Because she needed to hear it."

It occurred to me that Mr. Perkins, like me, was operating without a sheet of instructions.

More cars were pulling into the school, headlights blazing. The place was turning into a parking lot. Commuters who had been going home from San Jose to Santa Cruz had been forced to turn around when the landslides blocked the roads. Now they were trapped on the mountain, and they ended up at the school. Local people were coming, too, their houses destroyed or else they were simply afraid to stay home with aftershocks still trembling and no electricity.

Some people sat in their cars. Others wandered about.

In the dark of the mountain, there were spots of light: houses, burning. I could see five or six fires.

People — kids, parents, old folks — came up to Mr. Perkins and me and started talking. Sometimes I knew them; sometimes I didn't. Age didn't matter. Nobody was trying to impress anybody else or have power over them. We had all been reminded of a power much greater than ourselves. I told where I had been and how I had followed Lara out of the house, how Lara had somehow known that the quake was coming. Mr. Perkins told how he had been watching the tournament in the gymnasium when cracks snapped open in the floor and steel roofbeams started to groan and bow. Everybody, myself included, just had to tell their stories over and over again.

A teenage boy: "I was driving my truck. I thought I had a blowout."

An old woman: "I slept right through it. When I woke up, I couldn't believe what I saw."

A bearded man: "I rode my house down the hill like a sled. I don't know how I survived."

A girl: "I was swimming. Suddenly there was a four-foot wave. I thought somebody'd blown up the pool."

A woman with whiskey on her breath: "My house hardly moved. It's on bedrock. I had no idea how hard it was hitting everybody else."

Another woman: "It felt like somebody had jumped on my water bed. Only I wasn't *on* the water bed."

An old man: "I fell out of my rocking chair."

A man with bloodshot eyes: "It threw us all over and into each other. I was watching my wife fly by me smashing from one wall into the other. I was trying to grab her but couldn't. I finally got her on the third try before she flew out the window."

A boy: "I was on the toilet. It dumped me on the floor. And then it dumped on top of me."

A man with tattoos and a twitchy lip: "It was like Vietnam. Like a mortar attack."

A skinny woman with deep lines in her face and a Texas accent: "I was in Hurricane Hazel in Houston. I've been in fires. I've been in tornadoes. I've been robbed at gunpoint, but by God I've never felt anything like this."

As we spoke, the earth continued to vibrate beneath our feet. We were jumpy. And then, suddenly, we all became aware of a deep, distant sound.

LOOTING THE STORE

We all heard it: a deep *thwack thwack thwack*. We looked at each other. Was this another quake?

No. It was a helicopter. As it landed on the outfield by the baseball diamond, everybody cheered. We'd been discovered!

The pilot stayed in the helicopter while a man jumped out. Mr. Perkins walked toward him. I tagged along behind.

"We haven't heard from you all," the man said.

"Of course you haven't," Mr. Perkins said. "How could you?"

"I'm just here to see if you need anything."

Gwen said, "We have twenty-two people here who need to get to a hospital. If there are any hospitals left."

"We've got hospitals up and running," the man said. "I can't take anybody in this little bucket, but we'll send some bigger helicopters to evacuate the injured."

"We need some medical supplies," Gwen said. "I haven't even got a stethoscope."

"I'll send it," the man said.

"We need a generator," Mr. Perkins said. "And a ham radio so people can get out messages."

"I'll try to get one," the man said.

"We need a Porta Potti," I said, and everyone laughed.

The man said, "You'll have to wait until a truck can get through with that."

Soon they took off. About an hour later, another helicopter arrived, bringing supplies and taking away the first of the injured people. Gwen and Jennie helped load people while Mr. Perkins and I helped carry supplies. When parents were injured and had to be evacuated, the kids flew out with them. They were terrified.

After the third helicopter, Mr. Perkins grabbed my sleeve and motioned me to come with him. "We're going on a raid," he said.

"What do you mean?"

"We need food. Did you have dinner?"

"No."

"Neither did anybody else. You know what time it is?"

"No."

"Midnight."

Suddenly my stomach growled. All it needed was reminding.

I went with Mr. Perkins and three pickup trucks a couple miles down the road to the grocery store. The plate glass windows were broken. A sheriff's deputy was parked in front.

"Stay away from that store," he said.

"We were hoping to get some food," Mr. Perkins said. "I'll pay for it."

"I can't let you in there," the deputy said. "I've already arrested three looters."

So, I thought, some people *are* crazy.

"There are three *hundred* people at the school and none of them have had dinner. Isn't there some way you could — ?"

"I can't give you permission," the deputy said.

"But — "

"But I won't stop you, either. Keep a list of what you take. And don't touch any alcohol."

By flashlight, we looted the store. Everything had shaken off the shelves and onto the floor. With the power off, the milk and meat were going to spoil, anyway. The deputy beamed his car lights through the broken window. We filled one entire pickup with loaves of bread. We gathered every unbroken jar of peanut butter and jelly we could find. We packed eggs — the ones that weren't smashed — pancake mix, bacon, Danish, donuts, and orange juice, thinking ahead to breakfast. I found a box of Hershey's bars, thought of Jennie, but didn't take it. It didn't seem right to take something that wasn't necessary for nutrition or survival — although I bet Jennie would say chocolate *is* necessary. At least, necessary to people.

Back at the school we made hundreds of sandwiches.

A couple of people had built campfires on the playground. We were still dressed for the hot day, and now the night was cool.

Around one A.M. all the firefighters gathered at the school for a council. I saw the bald man with the mustache and beard whom I'd met at the fire station. By now my brain was spinning. I was exhausted. I needed sleep, but I was too wound up. The firefighters said sixteen houses had burned. Two helicopters had been fighting fires. With broken pipes and ruptured reservoirs, there seemed to be water everywhere except where you needed it. Most of the firefighters had been pulled off from fires to help people. They'd gone house to house for search and rescue.

No one had died.

We couldn't believe it. Everyone looked around at everyone else. All this destruction, and nobody on the mountain had been killed.

After the meeting, Mr. Perkins shook my hand. "Thanks for the help, Frances," he said. "Now I'm going home. If I still have one."

"You don't even know!"

He'd made the same decision as the firefighters. Helping people first. Homes were less important. Even his own.

The badly injured people had all been evacuated. I found Sidney sitting on a mat with Mrs. LaFeau and two other children. They were wrapped in a blanket. Jennie was beside them. She had a fresh, clean bandage around her neck. Nobody seemed able to sleep. I asked Mrs. LaFeau if she knew anything about her apartment. She said no. She said it didn't matter right now. I took a blanket and lay on my back, staring up at a few hazy stars. For a long time, I couldn't sleep.

Sidney snuggled right up against my side. In a few minutes, he was asleep. There was a smoky smell in the air. A half-moon, moody and red, hung in the sky.

I could see Jennie's profile in the moonlight. She hadn't met my eyes since Eric's house. I wanted to talk to her, to find out what was wrong now between her and me, but my brain felt too scrambled to tackle it head on.

A shudder ran through Jennie's body.

She was silently crying. Her tears caught the moonlight as they coursed down her face.

"Jennie?" I said. "Jen? Can you hear me?"

"I can hear you," she choked. "My batteries are like totally dead."

"You seem to know a lot about first aid."

"I'm certified. CPR, too."

"You've always liked that stuff. You used to wrap me in bandages. Remember?"

"I like health. I don't like accidents."

Unlike me, Jennie had always known what she wanted to be — though her goals kept changing. I could remember when she wanted to be a glass-blower. And then a U.S. senator. A chef in a choc-olate restaurant. And then an animal trainer in a circus. So I asked: "You want to be a nurse or something?"

She wiped her face with the back of her hand. "I'm going to be an obstetrician," she said. "And marry a rock musician."

"You'll have rock-and-roll babies."

"Not exactly." She seemed to have stopped crying. "You know what I think, though? I think every baby should come into the world feeling *welcome*. Feeling *loved*. When I'm an obstetrician, I want to greet each newborn baby with a Hershey's Kiss. Wouldn't that be cool? And maybe give them to the mother while she's in labor — while she's working *hard*. I might invent a whole new kind of medicine: chocolate therapy."

"I'm glad you're here," I said, and I meant it.

"Fran?"

"What?"

"Maybe it's bad for people, too. Not just dogs. They say it gives you zits. Do you think chocolate is an addiction, like cocaine or something?"

"No, Jennie."

"Maybe I should be a scientist. Like you want to be. I could study chocolate. How it works. What it does to your body. Maybe I could find a way to make it safe for dogs. Franny — do you think I killed those mice? All that time I was giving them birthday parties and stuffing them with chocolate cupcakes, do you think I was *poisoning* them?"

"No, Jen. They kept coming back. The same mice. We'd catch them again and again."

"Maybe it killed them slowly. Maybe it — like — *accumulated* in their bodies until they died in *agony*."

"Jennie, cut it out."

"I'm sorry."

"It's okay, Jennie."

"I didn't want to be here, you know. I didn't want to see you again."

"Jennie, don't —"

"I'm not saying that to hurt you. I'm just trying to be honest. Trying to sort things out. Trying to figure out what I know. I mean, I didn't even know that *chocolate* hurts *dogs*. Do I know *anything*?"

"You didn't do any harm to Lara, Jen. The dog is fine. Don't be so hard on yourself."

"I'm not worried about hurting the dog. I'm worried about *myself*. When my father left and then my mother moved — and you were gone — and everything was like totally *wrecked* — I mean, I just didn't want to be hurt anymore."

She was silent for a while. I was puzzling over the connection between divorce and chocolate and dogs.

After a while Jennie said, "I wanted to stay in Pomona. I didn't want to — like — reconnect. And I was awful."

"You weren't awful. Just . . ."

"Weird?"

"Yes. Weird."

"I'm sorry, Franny, but I was so afraid of what would happen. And then it happened. I knew it right away. I tried to shut it down, but I could feel it anyway."

"Feel what?"

90

"We were friends again."

"That was bad?"

"No. It was good. Which was bad. Because then I saw how you were with that guy, and I knew I was losing you to something I couldn't stop, and — "

"Jen, it isn't like that."

"It *is*. It *is*."

She was crying again.

I didn't know what to say. Friendship had been so much easier when all we had to deal with were mice and puppies. I did like Eric, but if anything was going to develop, it had a long way to go. Can't you be friends with a boy and still stay friends with a girl? *Nothing is simple*, Jennie had written. *And nothing lasts forever*.

Until today, I'd thought some things last forever: the laws of science. Earth is earth. Rock is rock. Now the earth and rocks had shifted beneath our feet.

I'll never be able to sleep, I thought to myself. Not after everything that's happened.

But I did. For a while.

In my sleep I heard my father's voice: "Yep. That's them. Thank you very much."

91

I opened my eyes. It was still night. The moon had moved high in the sky. And there stood my mother and father.

They kneeled down and gave me a hug. Sidney and Jennie slept on. Jennie's mother — Jerri — was kneeling over Jennie, stroking her hair.

My head was groggy. I was sleepy and happy and so very relieved to see them alive — and at the same time, disappointed. Surprised at the feeling. But definitely a little bit disappointed. Now I was just a kid again. "How'd you get here?"

"Back roads," my father said.

"We had to move a tree," my mother said. "It had fallen across the road."

"How could you move a tree?"

My father shrugged. "You never know what you can do until you have to do it."

"I know. We lifted a Volkswagen!"

They asked if we were all right. I said we were just dirty.

"What about her neck?" Jerri asked.

"Just a cut," I said.

They asked what had happened, and I tried to tell them briefly, but there was so much to tell that I felt like I was just babbling.

"Never mind," my mother said. "You can tell us later. Oh, Franny, I'm so glad to see you. You won't understand this, but when you're a parent, if you can't find your children, if you don't know what's happened to them, you just know that they're *dead*. You know it for a certainty. And at the same time you're frantic. You'll do anything. You can move *trees*. You have to find them."

I did understand. As a matter of fact, I knew exactly how she felt. Then I asked, "Have you seen the house?"

"No," my father said. "That's where I'm going next."

"Let's wait until morning," my mother said.

"I can't wait," my father said.

"I'll go with you," I said.

My mother stayed with Sidney and Jennie and Jerri.

We drove the dark road. I warned my father to watch for cracks.

"I know," he said. "We drove over them."

"There's one you can't drive over."

The big gap in the road had gotten even wider since I'd last seen it. We parked, took a flashlight from the glove box, and walked.

Around our house, tiny shards of glass glittered in the beam of the flashlight as if the stars had settled to rest on the earth. The night was silent except for a slight stirring in the trees.

My father walked all around the outside of the house. Below and across the road in the old, abandoned, waiting-to-fall-down shed, I saw the flicker of one candle flame. Sometimes homeless people slept in there. I wondered who it was. Tonight, many new people were homeless. Maybe, it occurred to me, maybe even *I* was homeless.

"Okay, that's it," my father said.

"How's the house?"

"We've got some problems."

"Will it fall down?"

"I don't think so. But I need a professional opinion."

"Don't you want to look inside?"

"Not tonight. Let's get some sleep."

As we drove back to the school, I asked what it was like at the baseball game. Did they feel it?

"Feel it? The whole stadium shook. At first I thought it was people stomping their feet. Then a chunk of concrete fell out of the upper deck and landed in the aisle right beside me. The lights went out. The scoreboard went blank. The public address system didn't work. Nobody knew what was happening. Finally a police car with a loudspeaker drove on to the field and told everybody to go home."

"Will there be school tomorrow?"

94

"No."

"Lara ran away."

My father squeezed my shoulder. "We'll find her."

Back in my blanket under the moon and the stars, I heard my parents whispering. My father was saying something about the foundation. Sidney rolled up close against me with his hair against my face. It smelled like an old sock. I turned my head away. I heard the drone of a generator and, far away, the thumping of a helicopter.

LARA

In the morning some people cooked pancakes and bacon over camp stoves. It was sort of social, like a pancake breakfast at the volunteer fire department, and sort of sad, like a soup kitchen. We ate quickly. I had a huge appetite. Sidney, even though my parents had returned, stayed at my side, clutching my belt loop in a death grip. Mrs. LaFeau was gone.

Jennie's mom seemed restless, not interested in what was happening on the mountain. It wasn't her home. She wanted to take Jennie and go back to Pomona, but she had driven up here with my parents and couldn't leave until they could take her to the airport. Again and again she said, "Do you think it's on television? It *has* to be." Their house had always had a TV blasting even when nobody seemed to be paying attention to it. I don't think Jerri would really believe that an earthquake had happened until she saw it on the tube. But for now, she had to stay with us. And so did Jennie.

Today, Jennie wore no headphones. She didn't talk to me at breakfast, but didn't avoid my eyes, either. She drank three cups of hot chocolate. She seemed tired.

So was I.

Usually my parents dawdle over coffee. Today they skipped it entirely. "Let's get out of here," my father said.

We drove down the road. Even in the car, Sidney held on to my pocket. We passed the house where the woman had been cursing her garden hose. Now there was nothing but a chimney and charcoal. There was a black scar on the trunk of the redwood tree, but I'd seen lots of trees with worse burns. They survive. We passed another house that looked more like a lumber pile. A man stood in the center of the heap over a mound of bricks, lifting handfuls of roof shingles and splintered pieces of wood.

My father looked worried. He stopped and called to the man: "Is somebody under that mess?"

The man shook his head. "Nobody was home." He took a deep breath. "Thank *goodness*." He spoke slowly. "I'm just looking for my wedding ring." He paused after each sentence, as if he could only think ahead by one small thought at a time. "I left it on the mantle." Pause. He pursed his lips. "Back when it was a mantle." Pause. He frowned. "There's nothing else worth saving." Pause. He scratched his ear. "The only good news is that nobody was hurt." Pause. He brightened slightly. "And that it didn't burn." Pause. He wiped his brow. "Some good person turned off the propane."

That was me. But I didn't say anything.

For a moment my father watched the man. He worked slowly, deliberately, sifting through rubble. "You seem so *calm*," my father said.

The man looked up. "Outside I'm philosophical," he said. "But inside I'm *boiling*."

We drove on. At the big new house next to Mr. Vanda's, a woman was now hauling an armful of clothing out to her Winnebago.

A man came out of the house. He, too, had an armful of clothing that he dropped inside the door of the Winnebago.

My father stopped the car. He knew them. They'd just moved here from New Jersey. "You folks okay?" he asked.

"We're fine," the woman said. "Physically, anyway."

"How's the house?"

"Lost a chimney," the man said. "And a few windows."

My father nodded at the piles of clothing in the Winnebago. "You going out to do laundry?"

The woman shook her head. "We're packing," she said. "We're getting out of here. Just as soon as the highway's clear, we'll be gone. We're leaving. Leaving California. Are you staying?"

My father looked surprised. "Of course," he said.

"Right here on this mountain?"

"Of course."

They stared, neither understanding how the other could even think of doing what he was doing.

Mr. Vanda's chickens were scratching around his yard. They seemed to be able to take care of themselves.

We parked near the crack where the road had split apart. Two men with tape measures were on opposite sides, and a woman was standing inside the gap jotting notes on a clipboard. On the pavement right next to the edge of the gash sat a thermos and a steaming cup of coffee. On the road they had spray-painted circles and lines with fluorescent paint and planted little red flags on stakes. They certainly hadn't wasted any time getting here and getting started.

"It's bigger than yesterday," I said to my father.

The woman looked up at me. "It is? How much?"

I studied it for a moment. "About half a foot," I said.

"Wider? Or deeper?"

"Wider. I can't really tell how deep it is."

She made a note on her clipboard and said, "When did you first see it?"

"Just a few minutes after the quake."

"Before the first aftershock?"

"Um. After."

"Before the second big one?"

"I'm not sure how big it was."

"There was a big aftershock — five point nine — about three minutes after the quake and another — five point two — about a half hour later."

During the first aftershock, Sidney and I had been sitting next to the house, wondering what to do. During the second one, we had been running to the fire station.

"I saw it after the first one, before the second one. How big was the earthquake?"

"We're calling it six point nine. But it might have been higher. We don't know yet."

Jennie said, "Are you a geologist?"

"Yes."

"Franny has a rock collection. Had. She makes earrings. See? She's wearing some right now. Agates. She found them on a beach."

Jennie had heard every word I'd said! She'd only pretended to be listening to her headphones.

I felt stupid having Jennie talk about my "rock collection" to a real scientist. All I'd had were some pretty stones.

The woman geologist, however, looked at me with interest. "I collect rocks, too," she said. "I

100

started when I was four years old. And look where it got me." She laughed. "Up to my neck in dirt. Watch out, or you'll turn into a geologist, too."

"I'd like to," I said. I meant it, too. I wanted to understand the forces that were shaking my life apart. Either that or else I wanted to make jewelry.

"Is this the fault line?" I asked. Mr. Perkins had explained about faults, where two sides of an earthquake slip in opposite directions.

The woman shook her head. "There's no offset," she said.

"Huh?" I said. Immediately I felt embarrassed for sounding so stupid. Mr. Perkins would say *Huh is a sound made by cattle. We are not cattle here, Frances.*

The geologist didn't seem to mind. "If it was a fault line, one side of the road wouldn't line up with the other. These two sides line up perfectly."

"Then what is it?"

"It's more like the separation at the top of a landslide, but that doesn't make sense either because the downhill side of the crack is slightly higher than the uphill side. Landslides don't go *up*. And there's no armchair scar."

"Huh? I mean — what?"

"A landslide leaves a scar on a hill that looks like an armchair. And we don't have that here."

She seemed used to explaining things — and seemed to enjoy it. She continued: "The fact is, we don't know *what* this crack is, and there's more cracks around here, too. I need to measure them and map them before the highway department comes along and fills them up. Then I'll look at the data and see if I can figure out what's going on."

"Is it safe, standing in there?"

"Oh, sure. If anything, it will get wider. Like you saw. Of course, maybe I shouldn't be so confident since I just told you I don't know why this fissure is here in the first place."

Someone had laid a board like a footbridge over the gap. We passed over it and walked toward our house.

Standing in our driveway was Eric. And Lara!

Lara came bounding up the driveway to greet us. Her fur was full of foxtails and stick-me-tights, but otherwise she was no worse for wear. Sidney grabbed her around the neck. Lara licked him and curled around and beat him with her wagging tail.

I wondered where she had spent the night. Even more, I wondered what she had sensed that made her whine and go trotting out of the house — leading us behind her — just two minutes before the earthquake struck.

102

Jennie got on her knees and with her fingers started combing and picking at Lara's fur. "I wish I could give you some M&M's, girl," she said.

Lara didn't need chocolate. She was simply glad to be back.

As she groomed Lara, Jennie stole glances at Eric. She seemed wary. Eric, in turn, nodded a greeting — which made Jennie look away. I'd told Eric a few things about Jennie — that she was going to visit me, that she was an old friend, that we used to give birthday parties to mice. I wondered what he was thinking.

"Eric," I asked, "where'd you find Lara?"

"I saw her going by my house this morning." He looked down and toed the ground with one shoe. He was a little shy. "So I ran outside — I mean, I thought maybe you were — I mean, I just happened to come out looking for the newspaper — but you weren't there — but I guess you know that — anyway, she came up to me and wagged her tail and seemed to want me to follow her, so I did. So here she is. I hope — uh — I mean, do you mind that I came over to your house?"

"Of course not. I'm glad. That is, I just happened to — you know — just happened to want you to do that."

Eric stepped over to Jennie, who was still kneeling by the dog.

"Uh . . . Jennie?"

She remained on her knees. She looked up at him cautiously.

"I — uh — I mean I just happen to have — uh — " He held out his hand. "Would you like this?"

On his palm was a somewhat mangled — but still wrapped — Hershey's bar. I'd told him about that aspect of Jennie, too.

Jennie stood up. Without a word, looking slightly afraid, slightly guilty, slightly embarrassed, she took the Hershey's bar. She opened the wrapping and broke off one square and put it in her mouth. She broke off another square, started to offer it to Lara, then — catching herself — pulled it back and ate it herself. Lara looked disappointed.

Eric turned to me. "So — what's new?"

I smiled. It felt good to smile. "Everything," I said. "And yet somehow, some things are still the same." And the things that were the same were making me smile. It felt good to be alive. Good to have Lara. Good to have my parents back. Good to be standing in the warm morning sun.

But a glance at the propane tank lying on its side

reminded me that not everything in my world was in such good repair.

My father and mother had already gone into the house. Eric said good-bye and headed for home. I followed my parents toward the house. Behind me I heard Jerri asking Jennie, "Does their TV work?"

I found my mother staring at the mess in the kitchen.

Sidney asked a question that may have seemed strange, but there was a good reason: "Will the raccoons come back?"

"Maybe they already have," my mother said. She knew what he was thinking. "From the looks of the kitchen, there's no way to tell."

We used to feed raccoons from the kitchen window. They'd climb up a redwood tree and out on a limb to get to the windowsill. Once, we'd left the window open a crack, and the coons had worked it open during the night. They ransacked the place. They tore open a bag of cornmeal, bit through a plastic two-liter bottle of root beer that dribbled all over the floor, broke a honey jar, stole a bag of granola, and left sticky footprints on the counter. Lara had slept right through it. She never barked.

We spent the morning working on the house. My mother and Jerri cleaned out the kitchen with a wheelbarrow. They filled six garbage bags, which I held open while Sidney was attached to my pants pocket. Then we swept and mopped.

And mopped.

And mopped. No matter how many times we mopped, the floor was still sticky.

My father made some changes to the plumbing so that we could get water from a hose faucet outside the garage. It came murky out of the tap. In one of the buckets that my mother filled, a live tadpole was swimming around. Dead insects spurted into another. "Don't drink it," she said.

Our water came from a cooperative water system. That is, each homeowner helped repair the pipes and maintain everything. The filter, my father said, was broken. He'd hiked up to check. We were sucking raw untreated water. And the little dam had failed. The reservoir was nearly empty.

I picked up my earrings and my rock collection, as much as I could find. Jennie helped. My little agates had sprayed all over the place. I set my dresser on its feet and stuffed the drawers back inside. My clothes were covered with slivers of broken window glass.

Under the bed Jennie found two AA batteries — and her face lit up.

"Oh, wow! Could I like borrow these?"

Sigh. What could I say? "Sure, Jennie."

On went the headphones.

Sidney detached himself from me long enough to gather all his stuffies and line them up on a shelf.

With Jennie I took the bedspreads outside and shook them. The little shards of glass still clung to the fabric. We found the linen trunk under a pile of clothes in the closet and pulled out clean bed-covers.

I repotted some plants that had jumped to the floor. I cleaned the bathroom. The door of the medicine cabinet had burst open, and everything had dropped into the sink.

My mother salvaged a loaf of bread and a jar of mayonnaise. With a can of tuna, that was lunch. She'd saved a bunch of other cans, too, though the outsides were covered with goo.

After lunch, my father said he had to find a working telephone. He said he might as well take Jerri and Jennie to the airport — if he could get through — and use the phone there.

"No," Jennie said.

We all stared at her.

"I'm not ready to go home," Jennie said. She was still wearing headphones. "I need — I want — I mean — Mother, you go."

"Jennie, you're missing school. I can't allow — "

"I'll make it up. Mother, this is totally important. I want to — you know — see this. I've never seen an earthquake before. This is history, what's happening here. It's on *television*."

She'd put it in words her mother could understand.

I would have preferred that Jennie wanted to stay to see more of me. Things had been seeming rather tentative since last night. At least, I told myself, if she wants to stay, she must be feeling somewhat comfortable with me. Eric had helped. His Hershey's bar had made a difference. Jennie was a little strange about chocolate. And I liked her for her strangeness.

Eric in his gentle way had known just how to get to her. I wondered if he knew how to get to me, too. And just how do you get to me, anyway? Did Eric know something about me that I didn't know? Maybe it was Lara. He used the dog to get to me. Was I that simple?

Anyway, I liked him. Just happened to.

Jerri was concerned that Jennie would be in the way of my parents with all the work that needed to be done, but my parents said they could use an extra pair of hands. Eventually, Jerri agreed to fly back without her. Jennie could stay through the rest of the week.

I still wasn't sure where I stood with Jennie. It had been a tumultuous visit so far in more ways than one. Nobody had asked if I wanted her to stay.

So I asked myself.

And the answer was Yes. I wanted her company. Headphones and all.

THE DEER

My mother searched through the garage, which was as much of a mess as any other part of the house. Everything on the worktable and the storage shelves had tumbled down. She found our big family camping tent and told me to help her set it up in the yard.

"Aren't we going to sleep in the house?"

"It's off the foundation," my mother said. She was frowning with worry. "Your father says it's worse than it was last night. We don't know if it's safe."

"It doesn't *look* that bad. You mean we might lose the *house*?"

My mother shook her head. "We might have already lost it."

"Then why were we *cleaning* it?"

My mother looked surprised. "Because," she said, "we wanted to."

Nobody had asked me if I wanted to clean a house that might be falling down anyway. When I thought about it, though, I was glad we had done it. I'd found most of my earrings. Half of my rocks. But I wouldn't have scrubbed the bathroom so thoroughly if I'd known we might abandon it.

Below us, new rocks were forming at that very

110

moment. I felt a little aftershock through my shoes. They came every hour or so. Sometimes I thought I might just be imagining that I felt something — some slight vibration in my toes or, if I was sitting, in the seat of my pants. Probably, sometimes, it *was* my imagination. We were all pretty jumpy. One person would say, "Did you feel that?" And we'd all look around nervously.

We set up the tent, unrolled pads, and spread out sleeping bags. Sidney moved a few of his stuffies into the tent. I found some clothes that had been buried away from the flying glass, loaned some to Jennie, and we changed.

Studying in the sideview mirror of the car, I brushed my hair — and noticed that it looked brown. I always think of my hair as red, but really it only looks that way when it's perfectly clean and catching the sun, as it had when Jennie first saw it on this visit.

Of course she remembered it as brown. I used to hate washing.

I'd changed. Here I was blaming all our differences on Jennie, but I had been growing up, too.

In clean clothes I felt fresh. We had a camp stove and folding chairs and a card table. I hung a Coleman lantern from the branch of a tree. It seemed as if we were living in *Swiss Family Robinson* —

salvaging our shipwreck and setting up a new life.

I actually found myself looking forward to the evening. The worst was over — or so I thought. We were together as a family — plus Jennie. I was operating on the theory that since Jennie had wanted to stay, it meant we were still friends. She just had a funny way of showing it, staying shut up in her headphones.

I liked camping. We would be under our wonderful redwood trees with our view of the sunset and the hills and the sea. I loved our mountain home — even if it was only a tent.

At night I saw flickering candlelight in the shed that was down the hill and across the road. I had to know who was in there. Sidney was still clinging to me like a tick, but I managed to slip away when my mother read him a story.

Jennie followed. She didn't ask where I was going or if she could come along. She simply came — silently, in headphones.

I clambered down the steep hillside and then ran across the road. A dirt driveway formed a circle around the shed. There was no way to hide. Cautiously, quietly, Jennie right behind me, I walked to the dirty glass window and peered through.

Inside were a man and a woman. She was pregnant. She had beautiful tawny skin and shining eyes. The man was short with the same dusky skin and a flat nose. By the light of two candles they were sharing some apples and a loaf of bread. As far as I could see, it was their only food. On the floor was a blanket spread over pine needles and grass.

I walked back across the road.

"Who are they?" Jennie asked from behind me.

"Homeless people," I said.

"Why are we spying on them?"

"I'm not spying on them. I just wanted to know who was there."

"They've got like *nothing*. And she — did you see her? She's totally pregnant."

I'd seen the man before. Mornings, he stood outside the little grocery store down the road. Some days, a dozen men would be standing there. Men in pickup trucks would come by and hire them for the day to dig ditches or cut insulation or clean out manure or do some other job that nobody else wanted to do.

We climbed back to our tent. It was crowded with the five of us. Sidney insisted that I lie down beside him. My mother read story after story until finally Sidney closed his eyes.

When he was asleep, I whispered to my mother

what I had seen in the shed. She turned to my father.

"John, can we help them?"

That was my mother. We'd been forced out of our house and into a tent — and she wanted to help other people.

"Let's talk to them in the morning," my father said.

"Good."

But morning, as it turned out, was a long time away.

Sometime during the night I felt a nasty jolt. At first I thought it was Sidney kicking me in his sleep, but then I heard the train roaring up the canyon. I heard groans from the house as if it were saying *Oh no, not again.* Then something snapped — the unmistakable sound of breaking wood. I sat up with a start. My father and mother and Jennie were sitting up, too.

We got up. We each had flashlights. We shined them on the house and saw that in the aftershock the old part had broken away from the new. The addition seemed to be straight while the old section — the part we had been living in — sagged at an angle.

My mother held on to my father. I held on to my

114

mother. The house of our dreams had split in half.

"I'm so *sorry*," Jennie said as if it were her fault.

"I'm glad we weren't sleeping in there," I said.

Sidney came stumbling out of the tent. "Make it *stop*," he said.

"I wish I could," my father said.

I was angry. I wanted to be mad at somebody. *Scream* at some fool. Punch and kick and yell at some horrible person who had caused this to happen. But there was nobody to blame. I thought of my great-grandfather who had always cursed the mayor for the San Francisco earthquake of 1906. Maybe, like me, he'd needed someone to blame.

I looked out over the hills. The moon was smaller tonight. Waning. Usually the lights of scattered houses dotted the dark hillsides, but without electricity the mountain was dark. Except for right below. Something was flickering in the old shed — flames, licking the window.

The shed was on fire!

We slipped and slid down the hill. By the time we got to the shed, there was nothing we could do. A candle must have fallen into the bedding of pine needles and dry grass. The walls had caught like kindling.

The man and the woman had disappeared. At

that moment they were hiding somewhere in the woods. If they had owned any possessions, all were now lost in the flames.

"I hope they aren't hurt," my mother said. "Would you try calling them?"

I was the only one in our family who knew any Spanish, and not much at that. "*¿Dónde están?*" I called out. Where are you?

No answer.

"Ask them if they're hurt."

"*¿Están bien?*" Are you all right?

Jennie knew the word for hurt. "*¿Heridos?*" she called.

No answer from the woods.

"They must be terrified. Tell them we want to help."

"*¡Deseamos ayudar!*"

In reply, there was only the screech of an owl and the crackle of the fire. In minutes, the shed had collapsed in a shower of sparks.

No fire truck ever arrived. The whole system had broken down. You were supposed to phone them, and then they were supposed to sound the siren to call the volunteer firefighters to the firehouse. We had no phones. And, I suppose, no electricity to power the siren. This was more like living in the year *eighteen* eighty-nine. Like the pioneers. Next, would we be making our own soap?

The shed became a glowing pile of coals. It was surrounded by plain dirt — the driveway — so there was no danger of the fire spreading. We watched it anyway for what seemed like hours.

"I wish we had marshmallows," Sidney said.

Finally, we returned to the tent. Tired as I was, it was hard going back to sleep. Everyone else dropped off. I lay awake. My nerves were on edge. One more aftershock and I'd go mad.

I don't know how long I lay awake. Gradually I became aware of a scuffling sound. It came closer. I thought it must be the man and woman from the shed. Maybe they were sneaking up on us. Maybe they wanted to rob us and kill us and steal our food. You can't lock a tent. I lay frozen with fear. I tried to tell myself that they had looked like gentle, loving people — not killers. Maybe they were hurt. Maybe they were limping to the tent for help. Wake up, Daddy. I couldn't make my voice work. The noise was just outside the tent. I had to do something. Move, body. I sat up. I shined my flashlight through the mosquito netting window.

I was nose to nose with a deer. A doe.

She froze in my flashlight beam. For a moment, I stared into those big wet eyes. Then I switched off the light.

In an instant, the doe had bolted. As she leaped, she struck a rope and shook the whole tent. Lara woke up and started barking. And now everyone else in the tent was awake.

"Make it *stop*," Sidney cried.

"It's all right," I said. "It's only a deer. She was checking us out."

It has come to this, I was thinking. We are as skittish as deer. And the doe was wishing us welcome. Welcome back to the natural world from which we once came.

JORGE AND MARGARITA

In the morning we stood in the new part of the house, examining the old. In the addition, the floor was still level, the walls were still true. The old house had sunk on one side so that the floor sloped down and away from us.

"Dad? Why did the two parts of the house come through so differently?"

"Bolts," he said.

He showed me how the new addition was bolted to the foundation with heavy threaded steel. Then we looked at the old part, where the wood had jumped right off the concrete with no bolts to hold it in place.

He took me inside the addition and pointed out some heavy metal anchors bolted to the corners of the wooden framing. "Hold-downs," he called them. Those plus the plywood walls kept the addition from shaking apart. The old part of the house had been built without hold-downs or plywood. "In fact," my father said, "I don't think plywood had even been invented yet."

Just a few small changes had made all the difference. I was amazed. Fascinated. I wanted to look at other houses and see which ones had bolts or hold-downs or plywood, but my father said we had work to do. He said he wanted to move everything out of the old house before it collapsed.

"Is it safe to go in there?" my mother asked.

"It's safer now than it will be later."

"What if there's another aftershock?"

"If you feel anything, run."

It wasn't safe. It was crazy. But we were desperate. We moved nervously and quickly. Our footsteps shook the floorboards as if we were creating aftershocks. Walls creaked as we passed them. I was scared that the whole house would collapse on top of me but was determined to rescue my clothes, my photo album, my rocks and earrings, and junky belongings that weren't worth risking my life for but which I was determined to save because I was angry at the moving earth. I wouldn't give in to the quake.

We gathered everything that was loose but left the furniture. Soon most of our possessions sat in a pile like the remains of a rummage sale on the plywood floor of the new addition. They were protected by a roof, but no windows or doors.

"Will the carpenters come back?" I asked.

"Only to get their tools," my father said. "We can't afford them now."

"Do we have insurance?"

"No. We couldn't get it. They won't insure

houses that aren't bolted to the foundation. Part of the plan with this new addition was to add bolts to the old foundation, but they hadn't done it yet. And the new part couldn't be insured until it was finished. If this earthquake had happened two or three months from now, we could've been covered."

"What are we going to do?"

"We'll have to do it ourselves." My father looked grim. "We'll have to tear down the old part of the house and finish the new. It will take a long time."

"I'll help," I said. "I'll do what I can."

"So will I," Sidney said.

"We'll all do what we can," my mother said.

We spoke bravely, but it felt hollow. My parents had jobs. How much time could they spend working on the house? Did they know how? Did they have all the tools? And how much help could Sidney and I give? We weren't carpenters. Not yet.

My father drove to the school, which was now the town's information and gossip center, to see what was new. I went exploring with Jennie and her headphones. She wasn't talking to me much. She'd become a silent companion. Sidney, of course, tagged along. Suddenly I had become more important to him than my mother. He reminded me of a duckling who had just cracked out of his

121

shell and started following the first animal he set eyes on. He still wasn't singing. Strangely, in spite of the content of his songs, I wished he felt like singing again.

The Winnebago was gone. The man and woman had gotten out. By now, they were probably out of California. Yet, their house had suffered less damage than most.

Their house had bolts. The right bolts. I was becoming fascinated by bolts. They seemed as basic as rocks — and more permanent.

I saw white vans from the phone company. A big blue truck from Pacific Gas & Electric was hoisting a man in a cherry picker to work on a line. I saw an orange dump truck coming to patch the road. These workers seemed like saviors to me. Their houses were probably damaged, too. Their children were scared. But they were out on the job, trying to put our world back together.

My father returned with a case of white cans. Four six-packs. "Beer cans," he said. "Full of water. There was a Budweiser truck up at the school handing them out. They canned water for us."

"Is it fizzy?"

"No. Just plain, pure water."

He said the Red Cross was setting up an emergency shelter at the school. It appeared likely that a couple hundred people would be living there for a while.

"Are we?" Sidney asked.

"No," my father answered. "We've got our home."

"But it's *broken*."

"It's still ours."

We were back at the tent, eating a lunch of jam sandwiches, sipping water from beer cans, when the pregnant woman appeared — the woman I'd seen in the shed. Her blouse was dirty and torn. She walked toward us slowly, cautiously, her eyes wide and her head bobbing on her neck like a deer's.

She clasped her hands together over her belly and leaned forward as if bowing. *"Por favor,"* she said. *"¿Tendrían un poco de comida? Lo que sea . . ."* She looked ready to jump and flee if we so much as cleared our throats.

My mother asked, "What's she saying?"

I translated: "She said, 'If you please, could you spare a little bit of food? Whatever you have . . .' "

"Ask her to join us," my mother said. "And her husband, too. Where is he?"

I tried, but I wasn't sure how to do the verb tense.

123

The woman raised her eyebrows. She looked unsure.

Then Jennie told me I'd said *father* instead of *husband*. No wonder the woman was puzzled.

"*Venga,*" I tried. "*Y su esposo. ¿Dónde está?*"

"*Allá.*" She pointed vaguely toward some trees.

"*Por favor, dígale que es bienvenido también.*"

She flashed a quick smile. "*Gracias.*" Then she turned and ran to the woods. She couldn't run fast. She was pretty far pregnant.

"Did you scare her away?" my mother asked.

"I think she's getting her husband. I *think* I invited him. I hope I didn't say something stupid."

A minute later she reappeared. The man walked behind her. He had no shirt. No shoes. Just pants.

They were short people. Even the man was no taller than me.

My mother held out the bread. "How do you say bread?" she asked me.

"*Pan.*"

"Do you want some *pan*?" She turned to me. "How do you say jam?"

"I don't know."

But the woman understood. "*Pan y dulce. ¡Maravilloso! ¡Gracias! ¡Muchas gracias!*"

We needed no translation of that. They grinned. The man shook my father's hand. They ate three sandwiches and each drank a can of beer water. My mother and father whispered to each other. My mother seemed earnest about something. My father was nodding his head eagerly.

Then the man said, formally, *''Estoy en deuda con ustedes.''* I am in debt to you.

I said, *''De nada.''* It's nothing. You're welcome.

My father said, "Ask them if they'll help us. I know they're afraid to go to the shelter. Tell them we have some clothes they can wear. I think your pants, Frances, will fit him better than mine. Ask him if he'll work with me. I can pay him something. Not a whole lot. But we can give them food. And shelter. We have another tent. And heaven knows, there's plenty of work to do."

It took me a while to figure out how to say all that. Eventually, I got through it. I left out the part about my pants, though. I thought he might refuse to wear them if he knew they came from a girl.

They agreed — with a lot of head nodding and flashing of teeth from the woman. The man was more cautious and distant.

I wasn't so sure, either. My parents were offering to let these people *live* with us. For how long? We didn't know them. They seemed nice enough, but we'd just lost half our house — the livable half —

and now we were going to share our space, our tents, with strangers. My mother considered herself an instant judge of character. I hoped she was right. But still . . .

Slowly it was dawning on me how much we had lost. Not only *things* — the windows, the aquarium, the stove — but our whole *life* had changed. All of our money, my father had told me, plus a lot of borrowed money had gone into the construction of the house. Now we needed more money to rebuild. I wondered: Are we now poor? Is that why we're inviting strangers to share our house — that is, our tents?

The man, Jorge, helped my father move furniture from the old house to the new. Though short, Jorge was strong. They even managed to push the refrigerator uphill. There was no place to plug it in — and no power if they could — but my father wanted to get everything out of the old house. He was expecting the worst.

Meanwhile my mother and the woman, Margarita, put together a makeshift kitchen next to the tent. Jennie stopped being my silent companion and started hanging around Margarita, watching her every move. She seemed fascinated. Sidney and I set up our other tent, the one Sidney and I usually slept in when we went camping, for

Jorge and Margarita. We put blankets and pillows inside.

For the rest of the afternoon my father and Jorge went to work on the water system. A whole crew of neighbors were trying to patch it back together. My mother sat down with Margarita — with Jennie nearby. Using me as a translator — and this was hard, even with a dictionary — my mother asked about the baby. When was it due?

I butchered the question, but Margarita understood. About a month, she said.

My mother asked what kind of medical care she had received.

I tried to translate, but Margarita didn't seem to understand. She shook her head.

"When did she last see a doctor?" my mother asked.

I translated the question.

Again Margarita shook her head. *"Nunca."*

"Never," I said.

My mother looked shocked. "Never?"

I repeated: *"¿Nunca? ¿Verdad?"*

Margarita nodded. *"En mi vida."* Never in my life.

"How old is she?"

That was easy to translate. It's one of the first things you learn in Spanish.

127

She answered: fifteen.

Now I couldn't believe I'd heard her right. *"¿Quince?"* Fifteen?

She wrote the number in the dirt.

She was just one year — but so much older — than me. Pregnant. Homeless.

How old was Jorge? my mother wanted to know.

Seventeen.

Where were they from?

El Salvador.

How did they get here?

Margarita lifted her eyes to the sky. She sighed. Long journey, she said. They were robbed. Walking, hiding, begging. Finally they had gotten help from a church. Mostly, she said, it was a *pesadilla* — a nightmare. She seemed to shudder at the thought.

I stared at Margarita. This woman just one year older than me had *walked* to California from El Salvador. She had known hardship that I could barely imagine. Fifteen. With experience written in her face by a whole lifetime of earthquakes of the spirit. And yet still from time to time I had caught a playful glint in her eye.

My mother had heard enough. She told me she was driving to the nearest working telephone to call her doctor and make an appointment for

Margarita. She told me to suggest to Margarita that she lie down and take a rest.

"She doesn't look like she wants to rest," I said.

"I know," my mother said. "She looks stronger than any of us."

I suggested it anyway, after my mother had gone. Margarita seemed unwilling to try it. She wanted to find work to do. Jennie frowned. She took Margarita by the hand. She led her like a goat to the door of the tent. I held the flap open. Jennie patted the blankets. She unrolled a bag of M&M's from her pocket, shook a few into her hand, and set them on the pillow.

Margarita shrugged. Then she grinned. She crawled into the tent where Sidney and I had slept on many a camping trip, ate the M&M's, curled on her side, nestled one pillow under her head, another under her belly, and — to my surprise — went out like a light.

THANK YOU FOR
WHAT WE HAVE

While Margarita slept, I walked to the road. Sidney, of course, came with me. Jennie stayed, sort of on guard over Margarita. Jennie had said she wanted to be an obstetrician. Maybe she was hoping Margarita would go into labor.

I couldn't get used to the idea that Margarita was just one year older than me. How could she be having a *baby*? She was just a teenager.

And yet she was so much more.

I'd felt like more than a teenager, too, until my parents came back. Now I was happy to be in their care. Maybe that was the difference. Margarita had no parents. She had no choice about growing up. I could do it at my own pace. And in these last couple of days, the pace had been fast.

The geologist whom I'd spoken with the day before had returned. This time she was working without helpers, but she wasn't alone. A television crew was filming her and pointing a long padded microphone in her direction. She was standing next to the crack in the road where she had planted little plastic flags and spray-painted lines and circles.

"I don't understand this rupture," she was saying. "It doesn't look like an earthquake fault. It doesn't look like a landslide, either."

Was Jerri watching this woman on television as I was watching her in person?

A man in the television crew — the one who was holding the microphone — asked her, "What were you hoping to find?"

"Offset," she said. "In the 1906 earthquake, the earth slipped as much as twenty feet along the fault line. That is, if you had a fence that went across the fault line before the quake, afterwards you had a broken fence with the two sides twenty feet apart. But in this earthquake, after all that shaking, we can't find *any* offset."

"What does that mean?" asked the man with the microphone.

The woman wiped her brow. She said, "It means, we don't know what happened here." She tapped her clipboard full of notes. "But we *will*."

"If you had to make a guess right now, what would you say?"

She thought a moment. It seemed to me that she already had a theory but was reluctant to say it. Finally, she gave in: "I'd guess that the energy of the earthquake concentrated in the ridgetop, even though the hypocenter was deeper than usual —

eleven miles below the surface. The ground simply shattered. It's called ridgetop spreading. The cracks on this ridge are like the cracks on a rising loaf of bread. Like stretch marks. It appears that the earth moved *up*, not over. It's as if the mountain shrugged its shoulders."

My mountain, Loma Prieta, had shrugged her shoulders. We may love her. But she obviously didn't care one way or the other about us.

"We won't have all the answers about what happened here for a long time," the geologist continued.

Suddenly she pointed at me.

"There," she said. "There's a geologist of the future."

Now the camera was aiming at me — and Sidney beside me. Was Jerri watching? Was the whole *world* watching?

"Someday this young girl with her rock collection will go off to college and then come back to this mountain and figure it all out."

I was embarrassed. I didn't know what to do with my hands. I smiled for the camera.

Sidney pretended to vomit.

I could have killed him. I could have killed the geologist, too, for putting me on the spot. But she was right. Someday, I hoped, I would figure it all out.

Jorge and my father returned dirty and tired from working on the water system. My mother returned with a bag of groceries. The store was open, though supplies were low. She said that the store manager had refused to take any money for the food we "looted" from them on the night of the quake. He made it a donation.

My mother had bought tortillas, cheese, a red onion, and a can of refried beans. She asked me, "What's Spanish for help?"

"*Ayudar,*" I said.

Margarita had just come out of the tent from her nap.

"*¿Ayudar?*" my mother said. "*¿Quesadillas?*"

It wasn't the right way to say it, but Margarita understood. "Okay," she said.

We must have looked surprised to hear her speak the English word.

She giggled.

"*¿Hablas inglés?*" I asked. Do you speak English?

"Okay," Margarita said.

"Why didn't you say so?"

Margarita stared at me blankly.

"Will you help my mother make quesadillas?"

The same blank stare.

"Do you speak English or don't you?"

Margarita grinned. "Okay," she said.

We went back to Spanish.

Margarita helped my mother make a sort of fried quesadillas. Jennie hovered on the sidelines. I stayed around to translate, but I wasn't needed. When my mother handed Margarita a knife and an onion, the meaning was obvious. "Okay," Margarita said, and she sliced. As they heated the tortillas in a frying pan, my mother handed the spatula to Margarita and raised her eyebrows questioningly. Margarita lifted a tortilla, inspected the bottom, and said, *"Perfecto."*

When dinner was ready, they both seemed proud of the result, although Margarita kept trying to explain that these were not at all what they call *quesadillas* in El Salvador. My mother just kept smiling, not understanding. Clearly she was taking a liking to Margarita. So was I. Margarita had a childish toothy grin (with crooked teeth) but the bearing of an older woman.

While my father washed his hands in water from the hose, he pointed out how much cleaner the water was, though the pressure was still low. He and Jorge and some neighbors had fixed the filter and shored up the dam as best they could. Apparently, they hadn't had a language problem, either. A shovel and a washed-out dam needed no translation. My father said Jorge hadn't spoken a word all afternoon. He seemed the strong, silent type. Also, he was wary. I bet he'd been cheated — betrayed — many a time.

It was wonderful to have clean water. You don't appreciate the simple things until you lose them.

I thought of Mr. Vanda. If he could have walked, he would have been up there helping to fix the dam, too. Unrehearsed. Fumbling. An everyday sort.

I thought of Sidney pretending to vomit on camera when the geologist was talking about me, and I was thinking that he was a very small hero indeed. But actually, I had to admit, I was glad that he was feeling at least a little better, that the old Sidney was coming back, the Sid whom I knew and . . . loved.

Yes.

I had to admit it. I loved the little creep. In the structure of our family, we were bolted.

We wouldn't all fit around the card table, so we spread a blanket on the ground and sat in a circle. Before we could eat, Margarita bowed her head and muttered a few words. Then she crossed herself.

"What did she say?" my mother asked.

I translated: "Bless you, Jesus, that we are alive and safe. Thank you for what we have."

My mother looked at our split-apart house. She looked down at the road, where a boulder still lay on the crushed car. She looked at the ashes of the shed that had once been home to Jorge and Margarita. She looked toward Mr. Vanda's yard, where there was no longer any house at all, just chickens scratching in the scorched earth.

She looked out over the ocean and up at our redwood trees standing so calmly in the rays of the setting sun. She looked at Sidney, who was fidgeting, waiting for a sign that he could dive into his food. Her eyes met mine, and I don't know what she saw. She looked at Jennie, who had removed her headphones for the meal. She looked at Jorge and my father, where beads of sweat had plowed clean tracks down their dirty brows and cheeks. She looked at little Margarita, with one hand resting on the shelf of her gigantic belly.

"Thank you," my mother said, "for all that we have."

* * *

Margarita had started a tradition. From then on, we started every meal with a thank-you for what we had. And on those following days, it seemed, beyond ourselves we had very little.

Friday morning right after breakfast a gray Jeep with an official county seal on the side pulled up at our house. Jorge and Margarita beat wings and disappeared like quail. Out of the Jeep stepped a man wearing a hard hat and carrying a clipboard. He took one brief look at our house and stapled a red tag to the doorframe.

It was condemned.

My father was furious. He blew up at the guy. He said that only the old part should be red-tagged and that we should be allowed to use the new addition.

Blowing up at a bureaucrat is not the way to get what you want.

The Jeep departed; Jorge and Margarita returned; my father fumed. The red tag remained.

A wind was picking up. The sky was a moody gray, growing blacker. Blown leaves were whipping against my legs.

And then it rained.

We sat in the tent. Jorge and Margarita stayed

in their separate tent, Margarita singing softly in Spanish — the same song, again and again. It sounded like a lullaby. Jorge remained silent. The raindrops sounded like fingernails tapping on a tabletop. The nylon roof shuddered in the wind. The sleeping bags got damp spots where they touched the walls. My mother's eyeglasses steamed over. From outside came the scent of wet earth; from inside, wet wool.

We read books. We talked. We got bored. We were too crowded. We got on each other's nerves.

When it came time for lunch, my mother couldn't face preparing food in the rain. My father told us all to get in the car — Jennie, Jorge, and Margarita, too.

"Where are we going?"

"Aunt Annette's."

There were seven of us — dirty, wet, smelly — packed into a five-seat car. I felt like a dust bowl refugee.

Aunt Annette lived in Cupertino in a suburban ranch house. It was like coming into a different world. She had heat. She had electric light. She had running hot water. Telephones. Cable TV. Clean carpets and chairs. Windows that closed. I took a shower. I put a load of clothes in the washing machine. I walked comfortably barefoot to the kitchen and found Jennie and Margarita mixing some dark batter.

"Brownies," Jennie said. "I'm showing Margarita how to make them. Can you believe she's never had a brownie in her life?"

I smiled. I was feeling relaxed. It had been a long time since I'd felt so clean and so calm.

"Jen," I said, "it's good to have you back."

Suddenly Jen looked serious. "Yeah, it was fun. I mean, to see you again. I mean, the earthquake wasn't fun. But, you know — "

"I know."

"These brownies are for you. And Margarita. And give one to Gwen, too, if you see her."

"You can give it yourself."

"No. That's what I'm trying to say, Fran."

"What?"

"I'm going home. Your father just called the airline. There's a flight in two hours."

Why now? "It's too soon," I said. "They shouldn't make you go. I bet I can talk them into letting you stay a couple more days. At least through the weekend. They shouldn't — "

"It was my idea," Jennie said.

I must have looked puzzled.

"I'm in the way," she said. "You don't need me here. And I found what I was staying for."

139

"You did?"

"I mean I've sort of like totally been sorting things out."

"You have?"

Jennie looked me square in the eye. "Say hi to Eric for me. Tell him I'm sorry I was such a jerk. Give him a brownie, too. Would you? I hope you give him lots of brownies. For the rest of your life."

"I'm not exactly ready to *marry* him," I said. I was embarrassed. My parents were hearing this. Sidney was hearing it. I was in for some teasing.

"I'm just saying it's okay if you do," Jennie said. "And okay if you don't. I mean, either way, if it's all right with you, we can still be friends. Right?"

"It's all right with me, Jennie. It's like totally all right."

She was wearing a shirt that she'd borrowed from me. I said she could keep it. She looked to me like the Jennie of old: taller, thinner, longer haired, but still a companion of mice and puppies — and pregnant teenagers. And I knew that if some emergency came up — for instance, if on the way to the airport we came upon a car accident — Jennie would want to leap out and give first aid or CPR or at least offer a brownie.

But we passed no accidents.

"Good-bye, Jennie," I said at the departure gate.

We hugged. She still smelled like butter and cocoa. "Thanks for your help. I know you'll be a good doctor someday."

"Obstetrician."

"Right."

Jennie looked one last time at me and Sidney, my mother and father, and at Jorge and Margarita, who had never been in an airport before and were huddled together, gaping and whispering. "Goodbye," Jennie said. "It's been like totally amazing."

Then she walked on to the plane.

Driving home, passing all the torn-apart houses, the landslides that had been crudely bulldozed to the side of the road, the leaning telephone poles, the flashing lights of trucks where people were working even in the rain at night to string up wires and clear fallen trees, my father said, "It looks like a war."

Coming back to our tents in the dark, in the wetness, I thought of the meaning of Loma Prieta. It's Spanish for Dark Hill. That night, it seemed very dark indeed.

"Let's move into the house," my father said. "The new part is safe. It may not have windows or doors, but at least it has a roof."

"But it's red-tagged," I said.

"I'm not going to stay out of my house just because the county is afraid I'm going to sue them or do something stupid."

So that night, we moved into the addition.

We camped on the plywood floor. From where I lay in my sleeping bag, I could see the sturdy bolts of the hold-down in one of the corners. It reassured me.

Some time in the dark of morning, I awoke fuzzy-headed from a strange dream hearing an even stranger sound. It came from the old part of the house. Muffled. Distant. A ringing.

I shined my flashlight. In a window frame I caught the yellow eyes of a raccoon. Like me, it seemed to cock its ear toward the sound. In a corner I saw the glint of the hold-down. In sleeping bags, all unaware of the sound, lay my parents and Sidney. Under blankets lay Jorge and Margarita, his arm draped over her belly. Curled against Sidney lay Lara the dog. All sleeping. Still the ringing. I stood up and walked to the edge of the addition. There was now a twelve-inch gap between the new and the old house with rain falling through, and I didn't dare step across. I shone the flashlight over the buckled floorboards past the crumbled walls with the smell of wet plaster dust stinging my nose — and there in the beam lay the source of

142

the sound. Our old avocado-green telephone was ringing its heart out.

We were connected again. We were back in civilization. Though I was afraid to walk across and pick up the handset, I stood and stared at the lovely old phone.

Finally, the ringing stopped.

I went back to my sleeping bag. The raccoon was gone from the windowframe. My family remained sleeping — a family that had grown to six people in an unfinished house that had split in half. The raindrops tapped. The hold-downs held. Bolts.

Good old bolts.

A NOTE FROM THE AUTHOR

The Loma Prieta earthquake of 1989, also known as the World Series earthquake, was eventually calculated at 7.1 on the Richter scale (although first estimates set it at 6.9). The damage to the Bay Bridge, the Cypress Freeway in Oakland, and the Marina District of San Francisco was widely reported. Not so well known was what happened in the small towns and mountains that were less accessible to the news media — though closer to the epicenter of the quake. I live in one of those small mountain communities.

The quake struck while I was swimming laps in a public pool. Suddenly I was bodysurfing as an oceanic wave picked me up and carried me toward the shallow end. Two children — thinking that water would be the safest place — came running to the pool and jumped in with their shoes and clothes on. I went home to find the volunteer fire department cleaning up the remains of my chimney.

I've repaired most of the damage to my house. There remains one cracked window to remind me of what happened — and will happen again.

I knew almost immediately that I would write about the Loma Prieta earthquake, but I had to wait several years before I was calm enough to handle the flood of memories and emotions that come to me whenever I think about it.

The rumble of a passing truck, unexpected, shaking the floorboards, makes my heart pound.

The story is fiction. That is, I made up the characters. A few of the words spoken come directly from quotes of real people in the *San Jose Mercury News*, but I put them in the mouths of imaginary characters.

I don't know who made up Sidney's "Joy to the World" song, but I want no credit for it. I overheard some children singing something similar, and I altered it to fit the story. The children had learned it from some other children. Such is the folk tradition.

For his kind help and background information, I wish to thank Dr. Kenneth P. Simpkins, former superintendent of the Loma Prieta Joint Union Elementary School District. My thanks also to Ray Wells of the United States Geological Survey, Mary Hancock, nurse, and to Guy Denues, Chief Officer, Loma Prieta Fire and Rescue — more heroes, both small and large.

146

ABOUT THE AUTHOR

Quake! is Joe Cottonwood's third book for Scholastic Hardcover. His other novels are *The Adventures of Boone Barnaby* and its companion book, *Danny Ain't*, winner of the 1993 Children's Literature Award presented by the Bay Area Book Reviewers Association.

Mr. Cottonwood lives in La Honda, California, has been married for over twenty-five years, and has three children.

Designed by Ursula Herzog

Composed by N.K. Graphics, Inc.,
Keene, New Hampshire,
in Meridien with display type
in Copperplate